THE TEN DOLLAR ROAD

*For Brittaney
the Best Nurse Here.
Love Ya
Roy E. Benningfield
Ben N. Field.*

THE TEN DOLLAR ROAD

Ben N. Field

Copyright © 2014 by Ben N. Field.

Library of Congress Control Number:		2014919375
ISBN:	Hardcover	978-1-5035-1032-6
	Softcover	978-1-5035-1034-0
	eBook	978-1-5035-1033-3

All rights reserved. No part of this book may be reproduced or transmitted in any form or by any means, electronic or mechanical, including photocopying, recording, or by any information storage and retrieval system, without permission in writing from the copyright owner.

This is a work of fiction. Names, characters, places and incidents either are the product of the author's imagination or are used fictitiously, and any resemblance to any actual persons, living or dead, events, or locales is entirely coincidental.

Any people depicted in stock imagery provided by Thinkstock are models, and such images are being used for illustrative purposes only.
Certain stock imagery © Thinkstock.

This book was printed in the United States of America.

Rev. date: 01/23/2015

To order additional copies of this book, contact:
Xlibris
1-888-795-4274
www.Xlibris.com
Orders@Xlibris.com
663625

ACKNOWLEDGMENTS

To all of my family who helped with this book, especially to my wife Olive who was my writing partner and without whom this book would have never been written.

OVERVIEW

Ben's grandfather ranched with his son's near Lytle, Texas. His son Tom, Ben's dad, bought a place in Peaceable Valley, Oklahoma. The Log schoolhouse that doubled as a church is still there. When Ben was in high school he was moved to Montana. In 1951 Ben enlisted in the air force and spent the next four years in uniform during the Korean conflict. He has spent his life with his wife Olive raising their four children. Now that he is retired he can follow his dream to write. He has lot's to draw from. His grandfather was one of the first to ranch in south Texas. Fighting Indians and boarder thieves to stay alive.

His father carried a six gun from about age twelve, following in the footsteps of his two older brothers who were professional gunslingers. Ben's background is rich in actual western facts. Many of the incidents relived in this story come from real life.

CHAPTER ONE

"Hot, ain't it?"

The two riders sat loosely in their saddles; watching the beehive of activity in the corrals and in the barn. Laborers using brushes applied white wash mixed with lye to the corral fence and the barn. A war was going on against the big green flies that were everywhere. Vile pests by the thousands, covered the poles surrounding the corrals, the stalls, and all else in the barn. They were making life miserable for animals and humans alike. They had bred in the big manure piles by the barn, manure now being transported by wagons, and emptied on a field about a half a mile away. Other roustabouts were white washing the barn whilst still others spread lye around the barn and across the corrals.

"Hot don't cover it", the other rider answered.

This afternoon the Texas sun blazed down over the ranch yard with punishing man- killing waves of heat. Out over the small creek that bordered the corrals small clouds of mosquitoes whined and circled searching for prey, their sensors alert for anything carrying blood. It was so hot the ranch hands had not been able to sleep; they had just sweltered in their bunks. Working from can see to after dark when they could no longer see; they were tired, with bloodshot eyes and sore muscles.

Even the sycamores seemed despondent with limp drooping leaves. A tall, sweating, broad shouldered, red headed kid, slender of waist and hips, was leaning against the water well in the yard. The well was the only structure on the ranch that looked permanent. Each rock skillfully placed producing a well-built and handsome addition to the Ranch yard. About fifteen feet in diameter, it not only had a windless with a long crank for lifting the bucket but it also had steps inside, going down about twenty feet to a series of shelves for food storage, on which you would find cream, butter, eggs, cured hams, as well as other foods needful of staying cool.

The ranch house was badly weathered; time had worked its destructive powers on the board frame l-shaped structure. Even so, it had an inviting look, the wide porch that encircled the house was shaded all a-round by tall gum, sycamore, and cypress trees. It was located on the bank of a year- round creek that was deep and wide with a heavy flow of water that was home to some big catfish and bass. The creek was alive with all kinds of bushes, berries, Mexican plumbs and nut trees. The distant barn was in better shape than the other buildings; the corrals built with care, longhorn strong and six foot high.

The red- headed boy leaning against the well was Matt Teal. Matt was intently watching a cat play with a mouse. The mouse caught and carried about fifty feet from the big barn door and was now between the paws of his tormentor. He had made a run for the barn and its safety twice, only to be disappointed each time and returned to be released again between the paws of the cat. His fat little sides were shaking from fright and the exertion of his escape attempt. He wasn't going to run again. He knew and accepted the inescapable fate that came with capture. However, the big cat had played this game before and had known the mouse would eventually refuse to run. He gave the poor trembling victim a couple of licks with his tongue as though to reassure him it was only a game, but the mouse still refused to run,

The cat, calm and sure of the outcome, licked his paw and waited, watching quietly until the mouse was no longer gasping for breath and the trembling had quieted to an occasional spasm. Suddenly the huge cat raised his paw and knocked him rolling. It was almost like last night. The south Texas town of Two Track didn't get many homesteaders traveling through, but last night there'd been a couple of nester wagons in town. One of the covered wagons belonged to a young farmer and his new wife. The other wagon was for the boy's folks. They said they were traveling through, but Matt's Pa, Bruiser, had always said you could not take chances on homesteaders. You needed to stomp on snakes and nesters when and where you found them, those were the words he lived by.

It had been a hard day, the heat of the sun, the animal heat from a hundred head of corralled critters, the stink of burning hair and hide from the use of branding irons as critter after critter was road branded; all added together to make their day almost unbearable. However, every day would be the same until all three thousand longhorns were ready for the trail. Three thousand critters whose body heat radiated enormous temperatures; every one of them contributing large green piles for the manure pile and wetting the earth around them, creating an unbelievable stench. When the sun finally went down and a light breeze blew in, his pa declared the last one to the Red Eye saloon was buying the first round of beer.

Pa lost and bought the first round. Matt figured it was on purpose but his brother Tucker said, "Don't ya believe it." Matt thought maybe Tucker did not know everything. He was proud of his pa, especially proud of his confident manner of being able to handle any situation that would have buckled a lesser man. His pa would take charge calmly solving each and every problem, straightening out the confusion while he was getting to the heart of the difficulty and quickly putting things right again. Time after time, he had seen pa handle stampedes, face cyclones, and flash floods, and all the other emergencies that can happen on a big south Texas ranch. They had fought Indians, desperados, rustlers and his pa had always found a way to win.

Even this race to be first to arrive at the Red Eye saloon went according to the way his pa planned it. Sometimes his brothers never knew they were being "handled", but Matt had figured it out and admired his pa for the way he controlled things. Pa always made things come out the way he wanted them too.

The Red Eye built of logs; five windows let the light in. The bar was a half log with the flat side up and planed smooth. A large rock fireplace covered half of one end. On cool nights, the Red Eye was warm and cozy, always clean and friendly. The number one rule was all disagreements were taken outside.

A few beers, some shade, and lots of friendly conversation put the boys in the mood for some fun. It was about then that the nesters drove their wagons into town. Wagon wheels and oxen have their own peculiar sound and the men inside the Red Eye saloon didn't have to look out the door to know what was out there. Bruiser's face turned ugly and mean as though the very sound of a homesteader's wagon was a personal affront to him. Beside him, Jake Teal, the oldest Teal son and the ranch foreman, laughed. Actually, it was more of a snarl, the kind a mean biting dog would make. All the Teal boys left their mugs on the bar and followed their pa across the rutted dirt road to the wagons. A farmer and his son drove them; sweat stained and squinty eyed from staring down a sunbaked trail all day. Weary, bone aching lines stood out in their dusty faces.

He grinned and held his hand up to the older homesteader. "Howdy, I'm Bruiser Teal, and these are my boys. Jake here is my oldest." Then he laughed. "All these others are too many to remember. Except Matt, that tall one over there, he's my youngest."

The farmer took Bruiser's hand; "I'm Peter Ward and that's my son Bud driving the other wagon."

Acting real friendly, Bruiser took the men over to the saloon where there were free drinks and lots more howdy's and such. Already pleased to be enjoying the light breeze of the night after such a miserable day of traveling, the homesteaders was plumb overwhelmed that they had lucked onto such friendly folks. "We just needed to rest the oxen a spell a-fore we moved on to set up camp." The old farmer's tires eyes told Bruiser everything about the kind of day they'd had. If'n he would have been anything except a homesteader Bruiser would 'have liked the man. The farmer had no idea what kind of folks he'd come across all he knew was they had not found such neighborliness since they had crossed into Texas.

Bruiser was slapping them on their backs and laying the good neighbor thing on real thick. Matt was at the bar standing next to Jake.

"Hey Jake."

Jake turned to Matt smiling. "Watch 'ya need, Matt? Ya want sump'em to drink. I've already settled that here, ya can do anything any other man can do here in this place."

"It ain't that. I was just wondered why we're wasting time with these dumb hay-shakers?"

"Aw, it ain't wasting time, boy. Pa is just having some fun with the ploughmen; then we will run 'em on down the road unless we can get 'em to fight."

"They couldn't fight ya Jake, ain't nobody could. It'd be better to just tell them to move on and keep moving."

"I guess the point is we always kill a few before we move them on, that way they pass the word on – don't go to Two Track. They don't cotton to nesters."

"That's a right good looking wife that boy has. Don't it bother you ta bring her that kind of misery?"

"I kill snakes when I see them and a man who steals my range is worse than a snake – so if I kill snakes, I gotta kill the thief who steals my property. Ya understand boy?"

"I reckon so." Matt sounded kind of doubtful.

Jake went back to the fancy girl he was fooling with and Matt turned to watch what the other boys were doing.

Herman owned the bar and cooked sizzling steaks and eggs for hungry men.

Over the bar, he had a naked oil painting of Ruth, who did some singing and dancing. Ruth was lying on a velvet blanket and it was obvious that Ruth, favored with extraordinary proportions, was beautiful, and was everything a woman ought to look like. All the personal feminine body parts were covered with clouds. Six years ago, Herman had married her. Not a cowboy in the country would ever comment on Ruth's unclothed condition. That nester boy said, "Woo--ee that's a woman!"

Herman grinned at him. "I will tell a man, cook? Why she can make biscuits that just float away."

The farmer started "that wasn't ..."

The hand standing next to him put a hand over his mouth. "Yes, it was. That's exactly what ya mean." The farmer kept on, "But ..."

Two ranch hands grabbed him and shoved him outside; when he came back, he was subdued, embarrassed, and a lot quieter.

The other cowboys had started Injun wrestling with some of the hands from the neighboring ranches. The less sober were drawing and firing at imaginary spiders on the far wall. The homesteaders started getting shaky and scared. "I reckon we'd best be on our way if'n the women folks are gonna have the kind of camp they're set on having tonight." the older man told Bruiser. "They are a want 'n to wash clothes and clean up a little." Bruiser laughed, and nodded his agreement. They made their way out with a lot of thank ya's and nice to meet ya's. Bruiser just laughed, shook their hands, and let them head for their wagons. Course the boys had to come outside and yell their so-longs and come a-gain and some of 'm was shooting at the stars.

Quietly Jake slipped his rope from off his saddle and tossed a loop over on the young nester that had been so vocal in his admiration of Ruth's picture and dragged him back to the saloon. The boys were whooping it up and carrying on like this was all in fun.

Then Bruiser took the rope off the farmer and let on like he was standing up for the poor squatters but, every time that boy got close to his wagon, somebody would rope him and pull him back. They kept this up until finally he just stood there. Less than thirty feet from safety, it might as well have been thirty miles.

He was not going to play their game no more. Both the women were in tears and begging Bruiser to make the men leave them alone so they could leave. Right then the young feller's pa pulled a rifle outta his wagon and yelled, "leave him alone or I'll start shooting." When he pulled the rifle, Jake's hand flashed his Colt. Other men had died the same way, men who had faced Jake with their guns out, so sure they had the drop on him, then Jake would draw, and they would die never having even seen the draw that killed them.

The old man fell right by his wagon in the dirt. Blood welled up and flowed over his shirt, his old woman was screaming as the light went out of his eyes. His boy was on his knees, tears flowing as he held his pa's head, whilst his young wife tried to hold and comfort her husband. Jake started for the boy but his young wife jumped to her feet and stood in front of her husband. She was visibly shaking, tears were running in streams through the dust and the dirt collected on her face while riding on a wagon box all day in a dirt whipping wind. The wet streaks on a dust darkened cheek made a startling frame for wet eyes that blazed in fury and hate, eyes that jolted Jake and made him involuntarily step back a couple of steps.

Her young arms folded, she stood against them all, bound and determined, and some scared, but stomp 'n mad. His ma, her wrinkled old face covered with tears, the pain in her heart clearly visible in her eyes, had moved in front of her son. Her skirt spread shielding her boy.

Jake sneered, "Ya gonna hide behind your woman's skirts, boy?" Nevertheless, the blood lust of the moment had stilled in silent admiration for the young woman. The roar of the pack had quieted to an unnatural silence, the drunken men that had spilled out of the saloon shifted nervously, watching Jake.

Jake backed into the watching circle uncertain how to get on with it. He wanted that sodbuster but the women were in the way. Bruiser said, almost kindly, "Every man has got to kill his own snakes, boy. Ya let your women stand in front of you and the rest of your life you'll never have no respect for yourself." Bruiser liked the looks of the younger woman and the advice he gave to the boy was the code he lived by. His disgust showed as he watched the cringing boy that kneeled on the ground trembling in fear. He actually felt sorry for the boy's wife; he figured she deserved a whole lot better than what she had. His ma reached down and took hold of his arm. "Don't listen to them. They just want ya to fight back so they can kill ya legal."

They'd left then, the boy carrying his pa to his wagon, sheltered by his wife and his ma. The wagons had rolled out driven by the women. The mood had changed, somber and quiet now; the Two Track men stood watching. When the last sound had died out one of the Lazy B men said, "Well, this sure has been fun. Like the cat said after she kissed the skunk, I've had all of this fun I kin stand," he paused, "Yup, I think I'll head back to the bunkhouse."

Matt had laughed last night and he laughed now, as he watched the cat bite the mouse's head off. He laughed because the cat and mouse was so much like what happened in town last night and he wished he had a chance to prove his skill with a Colt right in front of the whole town. This morning his mood to be somebody boosted after studying the manner the cat played with the mouse.

"Hey, Kid."

Matt winced. He did not like the men calling him "kid" but Sam Bass was the "old man" of the ranch. He had been his pa's first puncher and had been on the ranch ever since. He had taught Matt everything he knew about being a man. He didn't talk back to someone like Mr. Bass.

"Mr. Bass?" Matt responded and waited until Sam had wiped the sweat from his face, inwardly noting the dusty bandanna had left dirty marks across Mr. Bass's face at each swipe of his dusty neckerchief.

"What are ya finding to laugh at in this blamed heat?"

"I was laughing at that cat playing with the mouse he caught." Mr. Bass turned and watched the cat pull at the dead mouse.

"Ya found that old yeller cat funny? That's just a mean streak that all cats have."

"Not any meaner the way the rest of you acted last night. Old Yeller reminded me of the way y'all kept throwing a rope on that nester and dragging him back from his wagon."

Sam grinned, "I'd say that old nester and his boy picked a bad place to stop in. He should have pushed on."

"The way pa buttered him up there at the first and got him and his kid in the Red Eye, you'd a' thought he'd found a right good place to stop."

"Nesters can't be allowed to stop here, any more than we'd make a place for Indians. Bruiser has a fixed way of handling them. We kill all injuns and we don't allow nobody else to move in here. But I think last night was going too far."

Matt wrinkled up his forehead and let a small grin show. "Maybe you were just taken with the wife of that homesteader?"

Sam just laughed. "She was something, weren't she? Standing there in front of her man with her arms folded and her chin stuck out. I'd swear there was fire shooting out of her eyes."

"I knew that old man was a goner when I saw him drag that rifle out."

Sam nodded at the cat. "He didn't have no more chance than that mouse had with old Yeller there. Still and all, that boy is a lucky boy."

"How come ya say that?"

"A lot of young men would change places with him anytime to have a wife like her."

"She stretch's that dress in all the right places, but so does Alice over at the Red Eye.

Sam shook his head in disbelief.

"Boy, there is more to a woman than just her body. She's pretty, but her spunk and her loyalty and that fire in her eyes mean a lot more than pretty does!"

Tucker, Matt's second oldest brother walked up.

"Sam's right that was a mighty fine woman"

"I was right! Both of you was took with her."

"Not just with her, but I'd give a lot for a woman like that to have for a wife." Tucker was serious and his face showed it.

"Then get ya a woman, if'n ya want one. There are girls in town that needs a man."

"There ain't a decent girl around that would even speak to a Teal man. They have all been told we are the worst men in the world. That's why ya can't get a girlfriend. They've been told not to speak to you."

Matt dug his boot into the ground and looked off to the sky line. His jaw was set tight and eyes narrowed. "How come? I ain't done nothing to no girl."

Tucker watched and somehow the big brother in him felt a flash of pity.

"It ain't what you done, it's who you are. You are a Teal. That means ya come from a tough family. Folks are afraid of us."

"They ain't got no reason to be afraid of me. I ain't hurt nobody."

"It ain't what ya done; it's what ya could do if'n ya needed to. You are a Teal; that means you are one of the toughest fighters, and one of the quickest guns in South Texas. Everybody knows Pa. They know how well he trains all his boys to be ready to stand and fight."

"They were glad enough to have me when the Comanche's raided Two Track. Everybody was slapping me on the back and telling me how glad they were that I was there."

"They were glad you were there, but when there ain't no danger to 'em they think about what a rough outfit we are; and then they want to be shut of us. Then they want their girls to marry somebody from their church."

"Then I'll go to church."

"They don't cotton to most of us cowhands; by and large as a whole we're too rude and coarse and disrespectful."

"Ma went there."

"Uh-huh, so did you when you were little. They were plum glad when ya didn't come no more."

"How come?"

"Ma never seen nothin' ya did, you was always a good boy to her. She never saw the black eyes and bloody nose of the preacher's kid and you just couldn't leave him alone."

"He's a curly headed sissy. Who cares about him? If'n that's what they want for a man, let 'em have him."

"They don't want him for a man, Matt. They just make over him because he's the preacher's kid and they can feel important being seen with him. His pa is an important man in town."

"Even the little boys can whip him."

"I give up, kid. You just can't see that to some folks that ain't important, especially some cow-headed little bit in a dress. Town folk don't think the same as real people."

"I don't see a need for town people."

"Me neither, except when we need supplies, or when we're hurt or when we need clothes or mail and things like that."

Matt scuffed his boot in the sand. "I hate this place and I'm gonna leave one of these days."

Tucker chuckled. "Me too, I've been leaving for years now."

Matt whirled on his heels and stalked off.

"Where are you headed?"

"I'm going to the pond."

"If ya let pa or Jake see you, they'll find somethin' for you to do."

Matt grinned at him over his shoulder. "They're gonna have to chase me down and hog tie me if'n they want me."

CHAPTER TWO

Matt was at ease riding Mouse. Fifteen hands high, he was built for speed and yet he was muscular. He had proven he could run all night and still have enough staying power left to make it through the next day; showing his mixed Arabian and Morgan breeding. Gray was his color and he had been the best cutting horse in the country before he got too old for the heavy work. He had been Matt's special horse ever since and he could trust him. The way to the pond was old hat to Mouse and Matt could set and enjoy the ride without thinking about anything in general. A trail ran past the barn and corrals then along the creek that bordered the home place. There were tall oaks, gum trees, pecans, and bodarks. Mesquite and creosote brush grew as high as your chest. Black walnuts and berry bushes intermixed with the thorny brush covered both sides of the creek. After about a half a mile the trail cut north towards a hill covered mostly with cactus. Above that was the pond.

Matt's face creased in a frown. He'd told Tucker he was leaving' and it seemed right but he had to think about this. His pa had pointed him out last night as the youngest son, but one day soon, he meant to be thought of as a lot more than just the youngest Teal boy. He was sixteen and, in Two Track Texas, being sixteen made him a full-grown man. However, even being thought of as full grown, his reputation was tied to his family's name and how he was thought of at home, and at home, he was just the kid, ordered about by any of his older brothers. In town, he was known as Jake's little brother or as one of them "hard as nails "Teal boys.

To the local boys he was somebody to stay away from, even when he tried to hobnob with them, because he could turn on them in an eye blink. Even the dogs gave him a wide berth, having learned from experience that friendly pats on the head could quickly turn into a kick. To the local marshal, he was a genuine certainty to be trouble. To his dead Ma, he had been a good boy, but, to himself, he walked alone and in his dreams, he was the most dangerous man alive. Many times he'd thought of just leaving the ranch, he'd thought to himself that as long as he stayed on the ranch he'd always be that Teal boy, but if'n he took off, he'd be his own man, make his own way, and no-body would ever make light of him. On this sultry, hot, July day, he had spent the entire morning "staying put" and "out of sight. When the heat broke, his Pa was going to take a herd of three thousand of those long horns and trail 'em to the railhead in Kansas.

Bruiser Teal, as folks called him, was a hard independent man. His folks had taken him to Texas before it was Texas where his life had been tempered by living on a hard time ranch that was close to Mexico. The Teals was there when it was governed by Spain and hung on in 1836 when the Mexican army camped on the Rio Grande on the way to the

Alamo. Bandits, rustlers, Comanche, and Apaches all fought the Teals and lost.

Over time, Bruiser had been hardened into a callused merciless man. Every one of his five sons had been raised with the back of his hand or a fist. Folks said that old man Teal had beaten his wife to death. Most folks were willing to believe it, but nobody asked about it because Bruiser had killed a dozen men or more and was a dangerous man with a knife or gun. Matt and his brothers had been on the receiving end of their pa's savvy know-how for staying alive and his rock hard iron notion that his boys were needful of being just as hard as he was. He saw to it that they were; he never took excuses, come hell or high water, and they finished what they started. They had done him proud. Every one of his sons went whole hog with everything they had done.

The Teal ranch was a cactus-covered range inhabited by rattlesnakes, poison spiders, chiggers, copperheads, and other vipers. A land where every living thing would bite you, scratch you, or, like the chiggers, that dig in and live under your skin. The Teal spread had a creek running through it; it kept a good-sized pond filled full year round. It was not big enough to be called a lake, but it took a good swimmer to swim across and back without resting. It floated a good big log raft midway across and some catfish and perch made their home in its depths. Matt was the only one to spend time there, his pa and his brothers not seeing any point to spending their off time where there weren't no whiskey or women.

There was pretty near to sixty yards of open sand on the south end. Around the rest of the pond were tall grass or rocks and boulders. Pecan trees, black walnut, a few gum and

Mexican plum lined the banks. In the old days, the Indians used to camp here to make their yearly gather of nuts and berries. They'd get staggering drunk on the Mexican plumb and stayed until the last plum was ate. Away from the pond, there was mesquite and the heavy brush was so thick there was only one way to get to the pond. It was an old game trail that twisted and turned through the mesquite, and the cactus, clear up to where the high bank on the north side of the pond started. There the ground turned to slab rock, reddish in color and stepped like it had been carefully layered. The pond was completely hid from sight until the trail topped the bank. When Matt went there, he mostly stayed on the sandy side or on the raft because the cottonmouths liked it under the bigger rocks or in the tall wet grass.

However, he had explored the whole pond. He knew where there was a wash out behind the boulders where an underground creek or an even larger stream had at one time merged with the pond, creating a sizable cave that sloped downward below water level before opening into the depths of the pond, making the last twenty-five feet of the cave submerged in pond water.

The cave was his secret, it was impossible to see because a boulder had to be rolled to one side to expose the entrance. He figured he was the only one that knew about it besides an occasional snake. That was how he'd found the cave, he had chased a big moccasin into it. Thus, on this hot afternoon, the cat and mouse game settled, his talk with Tucker was on his mind and he decided the pond was where he was gonna spend the rest of the day.

CHAPTER THREE

The rider had been in the saddle all night and he was looking for a spot to rest. He had badly underestimated the will of that sheriff; he'd turned and twisted and backtracked and still they came. Twice he had laid back and ambushed them, he knew there were at least two of them that wouldn't ride any further. An ordinary posse would have given up by now. He'd been watching his back trail but hadn't seen hide nor hair of the men behind him. However, he knew they were back there. His horse, a big long legged roan, had run all night and didn't have a lot of run left in him. He knew he had to find something for his bleeding right side and a different horse if'n he could manage it. Mexico wasn't far now.

Turning from the trail, he pushed through the trees, looking for water. There are a lot of creeks in this country and he needed one. Someone would have to be a real tracker to follow him in amongst all these trees, brush and such. "It's time to rest "he muttered," I must be in worse shape than I figured on."

The stream he came on to wasn't but a short jump across but it appeared to be several feet deep. The roan, stripped of the saddle and pack, rolled back and forth on his back;

squiggled awhile with all four legs in the air and neighed softly before returning to his feet to find enough to feed on. The rider, a man in his late twenties, was lean and hard, broad across the shoulders and skinny from the waistline on down. He limped to the stream on a bad leg busted years ago. His face was leathered by the sun with eyes permanently wrinkled at the corners caused by a lifetime of riding the range in the Texas sun.

Kneeling he washed the hole in his side and, taking his knife, he stripped some inner bark from a willow. Mixing it with moss and some whiskey from a canteen, he spread it across the wound as a poultice. Putting some small dry sticks together, he built a fire, knowing the trees would keep what little smoke there was from being seen. There were some blue flowered plants he seeped in hot water and drank the tea because he'd heard it would help the inflammation. Taking a swallow of whisky eased the pain in his side but it also tapered off his sharpness. Nevertheless, for a few hours relief from the gnawing pain, he was willing to take a chance that they couldn't find him here. Hot water washed the blood away and the poultice was working on the wound. He repacked his possibles so his pans and coffee and camp stuff would be ready if'n he had to take outta here in a hurry. He stretched out on his bedroll. "For just a little bit," he told himself.

It was close to night when somewhere in his subconscious a warning was interrupting his rest. Even as tired as he was, the built in sentry that he had developed from continuous watchfulness was pushing him into consciousness. A twig snapped, startled he grabbed for where his gun had been.

"Easy there, partner," Matt spoke softly. He was setting by the fire.

"I took your shoot 'n irons so you wouldn't wake up throwing' lead. Matt's own forty-four was in his hand. A broken dry twig lay at his feet. Matt hadn't stayed at the pond; he'd saw the rider push his way in by the creek and, figuring the bunch of riders coming for a posse; he'd decided to horn in. No special reason, it was just something to do.

The bandit glanced around. "Where's the rest of the posse?"

Matt grinned, "They lost your trail about a mile back and was heading' to Mexico fast as they could go. Started as soon as they heard you was headed that a-way."

"How'd they hear that?"

"I told them."

"All right, you got me boy, but what do ya aim to do with me?"

"They said ya robbed the bank in San Antonio. I reckon that's so?"

"You already know that I did."

"Uh-huh, and I already counted the money. You and me are gonna ride in to see the sheriff. There's a hundred dollar reward for you according to the deputy leaden' the posse."

The man laughed, "a hundred dollars! You are going to turn over more than five thousand for a piddling hundred dollar reward?"

"I ain't a thief and I ain't got no use for a hombre that is a thief."

"Then ya sure ain't got no use for that bank that I took the money from cause they plumb stole my place and all I had.

Look at me boy, my name is Johnny Tieg, and I'm a good man, my wife and babies are settin' in a wagon on the street in San Antonio with no money and no hope if'n I don't get back. All I did was taken back what he stole from me so I could make a new start somewhere."

"I don't reckon that robbing and stealing' is the way to support your family. If'n getting' even was what you wanted ya could have called that banker out and shot him."

"Bankers don't wear guns! He'd just laugh, 'cause a banker ain't a man anyway."

"Ya can't rob a bank and get away with it just because ya got a wife and kids. It ain't right no matter what he done to you."

"All I know is that my wife and kids is setting' in a wagon with no money and no body to care. If'n ya want my hide I can't stop you. They'll hang me because some of that posse got too eager and there's a couple of them dead. When my wife and kids are starving' it'll be partly because you decided to turn me in. You go watch her starve because she's too much a good woman to turn bad and there ain't no other way for a white woman to start with nothing' and make a living' in Texas. I ain't fooling' they ain't even got enough money to get something to eat. She ain't got no folks."

Matt set there with his gun on him and doubt hung on him like a cloud, he'd never seen a grown man beg before. It weren't the Teal way. "Pears to me like you should have thought on that before ya took to robbing and stealing."

"If your so blame worried about that banker's money, then take the money back to him, get your hundred dollars, and be proud of yourself."

"That weren't the banker's money; it belonged to the folks who put the money in that bank. All kinds of folks who depend on that money you stole." Matt's tone of voice left no doubt, he didn't believe there existed a reason for robbing the bank.

"If'n you're done preaching at me, I'm leaving or you're going to have to kill me 'cause I'm going to see about my wife and killing me is the only way to stop me." With that declaration, Johnny started loading his horse. Matt tossed him his gun. "Here put this on." He looked at Matt disbelieving "Put it on," Matt's chin clinched, "If'n I got to kill you it'll be with a gun in your hand."

Johnny held the holster and stared at Matt. "No sir'ee, I ain't gonna kill a kid. I ain't that low. You just shoot me, boy, 'cause that's all there is left."

"I reckon I will if'n you make me. It's either put that gun on or start riding for town."

"I'm leaving, Boy, you just do what ya think is right." With that he hung his gun across the saddle horn and picked up the moneybag. "See ya."

Matt watched as he turned his horse. He weren't gonna let him just ride away.

"You better do it like I told you."

"I done told you boy, I got a wife and kids and I'm going to go see about them!"

He turned his horse and kicked it into a run. Matt shot him; he aimed for the right shoulder and knocked him out of his saddle. He bounced plumb hard cause that roan horse had really been moving. His arm was all twisted under him, he was twisting, and moaning, he looked at Matt.

"I could have killed you boy, and then you did this to me! What kind of coyote are you?"

"Your dreaming if'n you figure you could've took me."

"Boy you're too blame ignorant to even understand. Have you ever been in a shoot-out?"

Matt never answered him, he just went on tying the bank bag to his saddle; a gray squirrel with bad timing left one tree, ran by the injured outlaw and jumped for the next tree. Matt's hand flashed and the little squirrel collapsed into a headless bundle at the base of the tree. He inserted a fresh cartridge before returning the colt to his holster. The bandit's eyes widen monetarily but made no other reaction. Matt smiled; he'd seen the eyes move. He didn't need to say anything else and the man on the ground didn't pursue the matter any further. Matt tried putting him on the roan but the feller passed out. So he took him to town across the saddle, face down and tied on. When Matt got to town, he tied up the horses at the hitch rail in front of the sheriff's office. The sheriff stepped out onto the boardwalk, a cautious question in his eyes. Matt told the sheriff what happened and what he'd been told; that the man had a wife waiting for him. "That just ain't true Matt, he's an outlaw, I've got a poster on him and he ain't married and don't have kids."

The sheriff paid him his hundred dollars "You could've took the doc out to him, there weren't no hurry. There was no reason to make a man hurt that much."

Matt shrugged. "He's gonna hang anyway, what difference does it make."

The sheriff and the doctor watched him ride off. "That kid is about as cold as ya can get. He's got no more feelings than some Apache injun."

The doctor answered, "The whole family's like that. I took care of his ma when she was dying, none of them acted like they cared."

"Did she really get drug by that horse, you think?"

"Who knows, she was really beat up; it could've been either way. There was no way to prove different."

"They are really a tough outfit."

"The worst I've ever seen. Old Bruiser has a hard code, them boys have been raised to follow it and I reckon one of' them would die before they'd break it."

"If they did somehow break his code he'd probable shoot them his own self."

"Probably," doc laughed. "I got to get back to my office, if that fellow needs more medicine call me"

And with that, he left, but the thought of how cold Matt had acted stayed with him and in the telling of it later, it grew with each new tale.

Matt went back to the pond; he didn't want to go back to the ranch because it was still hot and someone would surely want him to work in this heat. He had a belligerent hostile feeling and didn't want to be around where people could ask stupid questions about the shooting. For a while he had been almost floating he felt so powerful but the implied criticism had drug his powerful feelings to angry ones.

The pond didn't provide the lazy easygoing feelings he usually felt when he went there. Inside he was still bristling with indignation. He had the feeling of being about to erupt like a volcano and the usually soothing gentle rocking of the raft did not choke off nor still the turmoil within. He still felt the rebuke of the sheriff and resented what he felt was the unfairness of his judgment of Matt's handling the capture. "He's headed for the gallows anyway, "muttered Matt "What makes the difference how he was brought in. He was just jealous because I caught him." Matt figured he had the right of it but he still didn't feel any better about it. "Blame sheriff had to say something and ruin it for me. Someday I'll fix him."

With the promised revenge, Matt decided just to head back to the ranch.

Tucker had been in" Two Track" after some smoking tobacco and had already taken word home about Matt and the owl hoot he'd captured. So when Matt come, in they already knowed all about it. His pa took him outside, "if'n something like that comes up again I'd rather ya stayed out of it. I don't hold with butt 'in someone else's business and you made an enemy where ya didn't have to. No telling how many friends he has that will want to get even. And ya didn't need to back shoot him; that looks bad to just about everybody." Matt started to defend himself but his pa just laid a hand on his shoulder and he knew to keep his mouth shut.

"Yes sir, I won't do noth'in like that again." Matt flung himself in Mouse's saddle and kicked the gray into a run. His hurt feelings needed space and time.

CHAPTER FOUR

Matt was sullen and told himself he really was leaving. They never thought much of him around here anyway. What Tucker had said about leaving, bothered Matt. It had been several weeks ago but somehow he couldn't forget it. Tucker had said he'd been leaving for years. Why hadn't he just left if he wanted to? Matt wanted to strike out on his own; he couldn't see spending his life in a place like Two Track. His Ma had hated it here, she had told him her dream was too one day go back to Tennessee where she had family. He didn't want to be like Tucker and always someday be going to leave. Tucker wasn't no more than any hired hand on the ranch, none of them were, not even Jake who was foreman and drew foreman's pay. Bruiser owned the ranch and made all the decisions, paid all of them cowhand's wages. Why shouldn't any of them leave and work elsewhere if'n they wanted. Tucker had plenty of money saved; he was notorious for pinching pennies. Matt reckoned he him-self had plenty. His pa put his wages in the bank for him in Matt's own name. First thing he ought to do was go see how much he had. He'd never drawn a penny out. Anything he needed he just told Pa and Pa would get it for him and take it out of his wages. So he had the hundred dollars he'd just got and about three years wages less some boots and other stuff he'd bought. What was left should come to about nine hundred plus the hundred he had, about a thousand plus. He had his own outfit and Mouse. He reckoned that was plenty. First though he better check and see exactly how much money he had in the bank. Putting feet to thought he saddled Mouse and headed for town.

The bank was small, but built outta brick with a teller's cage and a large imposing safe behind the cage. The banker's smile was friendly; "yes Matt had an account there." His balance was about what Matt had figured.

"Did you want to withdraw any?" The banker was good humored, jovial and was obviously very eager to help.

"No." He shook his head; he needed time to make a plan.

"Matt this bank is here to help and if you ever need us we'll be here for you."

"Thank you sir; I'll be sure to let you know."

He smiled to himself; it tickled him that he had thought of being so polite. I'll just bet that banker wouldn't be half that friendly if'n my pa wasn't the biggest depositor of the bank. Still he was proud of being so polite; it was a new experience.

The banker watched him from the window thinking "how nice that young man was; Bruiser had given him good training and was raising a good youngster, he must remember to congratulate Bruiser when he came in again."

Now Matt didn't know what to do or if he did decide to leave, how was he going to go about it?

What would his pa say? What if he got mad? Matt didn't like the thought of Bruiser being mad at him. He could never know for sure how his pa was gonna take something. Sometimes he'd be real understanding and other times he'd blowup over nothing at all. Matt had a bad feeling about this, his pa might take it as a betrayal of the family or as biting the hand that had fed him and get real mad. If Tucker was so jittery about leaving that he couldn't make his mind up to go; there must be a reason. Could be that he was afraid of how pa would take it. Nobody wanted to be on the bad side of pa. He decided to wait awhile till it seemed to be the right time to bring it up.

It was a right busy time for the ranch. They were cutting hay, and in addition to the regular ranch work they were making a gather for a drive to the railhead in Kansas. There was a strip of land by the creek they was using for a holding ground that was already holding several thousand head, with more being added every day. Those longhorns were discontent, mad and upset. Ever last living one of them wanted to go back to his regular stomping ground. Riders were kept busy around the clock keeping them bunched together. Matt was doing a lot of night herding, this made long hours in the saddle pushing back critters that was trying to leave. He was too tired to worry about leaving his own-self; he was too busy to think about it.

Right at this moment he was following the tracts of a big old bull. He knew it was a bull partly because of the depth of the tract and because the tracts were blunt toed on all four imprints. The horns were so wide as to have disturbed the brush to widths of more than six feet. Matt pulled up, deciding to let him go. Sometimes the older wild ones would just lie down and refuse to move and he didn't feel like dealing with a sullen old bull. They had a strong will that could not be matched by any other animal he'd ever heard of. Those big older cows were meaner; they carried a full load of mean and fight all the time. There was too many critters out there to spend so much time with one determined old bull. Matt spotted another runaway and kicked his mount into pursuit. Jake would watch him and now and again chuckle to his-self. He knew the signs of discontent and he knew the boy was thinking things over. The best thing to do for Matt right now was to keep him busy.

The Teal ranch was hiring riders and roustabouts. The corrals were being cleaned in an effort to reduce the population of the big green flies that swarmed the horse manure. The corral posts and rails were covered so heavy with them you couldn't see the wood. They covered the barns, and even worse they were in the house. Bruiser had declared war on them and white lye was being spread wherever it was possible. It was on one of Matt's infrequent trips back to the ranch that he saw Tim, one of the kids from town working the shovel and wheelbarrow. Tim was close to Matt's age and was one of the few that were friendly to Matt. He weren't wearing a shirt; sweat was running in streams, he was covered with dirt, lime, and sweat, and swatting at flies. Matt hadn't known pa had hired on anybody his own age. He was surprised because Bruiser was notorious for being down on town kids.

Tim looked up and saw Matt setting at ease on his saddle and grinned, "Trade you places."

"Not me, I've done at lot of that already this summer."

Matt pulled his water bag and offered it to Tim, "Want a drink?"

Tim took a long swig and splashed some water on his face, "You folks sure got a big place here."

"We been here for a long time, it didn't start out like this."

"I reckon so, but you sure are lucky to belong to a family that has something. My folks don't have nothing and probably never will."

Matt sat still and watched Tim not knowing what to say. He weren't used to hearing anyone downgrade his own family. Finally he said. "It ain't always been so good." With that he turned and rode on up to the ranch. He didn't have any friends and Tim had been so friendly. Without knowing why; Matt felt a need to do something for Tim. Jake was standing there with Bruiser and they both looked up as Matt rode up in front of them.

"Jake could you give that new kid, the one working in the corral, a night herding job with me? I'd like working with someone my own age for a change."

Jake was surprised, Bruiser started to give an angry answer but Jake stopped him with a raised hand. "Can he handle it?"

"He can ride the rest he can learn. I'll help him."

"Will you be responsible for him?"

"I'll be responsible for him." Matt responded his face showing his earnestness.

"Send him on up to the house; I'll give him a try on your say so."

Matt rode after Tim. His word had counted with Jake and the feeling was good.

"How come you to do a fool thing like that?" Bruiser demanded, "We don't have the time to fool with kids."

Jake shook his head. "You're forgetting Matt's not a kid, He's also a full member of this family. Ya keep on treating him like a kid and he'll ride off one of these days, he's already been thinking on it."

"He ain't going no-where I'll stop that!"

Jake stared at his pa. "And that would make him want to stay?"

Bruiser snorted, "Why would he even want to leave, he's got it all right here."

"What he's got is a riding job at regular wages just like at any other ranch, he earns everything he gets same as anywhere else. Other than being with family it's no different than working anywhere else. Except no one else would treat him like a kid. I'll tell you something else, Tucker and some of the others are thinking on leaving."

Bruiser swelled up, his face mottled with anger. "If'n they don't appreciate what they've got and family don't mean nothing to them then let them go!"

Jake rocked back on the back legs of his chair trying to keep control of his temper, "How much does family mean to you. You better think about that cause you could end up with no family!"

Bruiser stood up and glared at Jake, "You too?"

"Why not" answered Jake. "We've got nothing here but a job, I can ramrod for any number of ranch's. I'm telling you if you don't start treating your boys with more respect and making this ranch mean more to them you're not going to have a family."

Bruiser turned and stomped out. Jake watched him ride off not knowing where he was going but wondering if he understood any of what he had told him. If he could have watched him all the way, he'd of seen Bruiser at his own pa's grave site. Just setting, resting his head on his knees. He'd dealt with rustlers, Indians, weather and bad cattle markets, now would his own boys turn on him? This seemed too much for him to handle. He'd worked for half wages from his pa and was blamed glad to get them. He'd of worked for nothing if he'd of had to, for just the sake of the family. It had taken all of them working together to build a ranch. His two brothers had died fighting for the ranch, his ma had worked her-self to death, and his pa hadn't lived to know anything but hard times and death. These boys wanted it all handed to them. He'd been the one to really build this ranch after his pa had been killed; he'd stayed when it had looked impossible, when wages somewhere else would have been better. Sometimes the hands had got paid whilst he got nothing. It weren't easy when the ranch hands could go get a beer and he couldn't because in order to pay them he had to go without any money for his self.

Now it was because he had sense enough to save a lot of hard Yankee dollars before the war when the ranch was paying good that they had money to run on. He'd kept his head while the rest of the south had gone crazy over the war. Hard money was scarce in Texas but he had plenty. Not in the bank where everybody knew your business, but here on the ranch, hid in a nice safe place. Those boys had never known hard times; they never knew what it was like to stay on year after year to back up your family when there weren't no money. To Bruiser family was everything that was important.

This was one of the few times he ever let his guard down, if he'd been as watchful as usual he might have known about the shooter with the sharpshooter rifle and a scope. The killer was on a small rise almost a quarter of a mile away. Bruiser was centered in his glass; he set the yardage by experience. He wasn't worried about missing; he hadn't missed a shot like this in a very long time. As long as his target didn't move he was a goner. Gently he applied trigger pressure until the firing pin snapped. The Sharps rifle and the telescoping glass were from the War Between the States, the skill to use it had been sharpened by his years of constant usage as a sharp shooter for Col. Berdan's sharp shooters during the war. Bruiser never heard the shot, never felt the pain.

The shooter stood up and wiped his weapon off, another fine shot and another five hundred earned. Smiling he mounted his horse and rode towards the river, in less than an hour he was in Mexico.

CHAPTER FIVE

It was a somber family meeting. The kitchen table was covered with a new oilcloth; a pot of coffee sat in the middle of the table and around it sat all the Teal boys. Jake sat at the one end and Tucker at the other; the young men were wearing stern somber grim faces. On the table by the coffee pot were the account books and two large leather bags opened at the top and showing the contents, some gold coins had spilled out and lay beside the bags on the table. James, who handled the business affairs of the ranch, brought them up to date on the finances. There were some hard choices to be made. All of the five Teal boys wanted to go after the bushwhacker that had killed their pa. But a ranch as big as the Teal ranch couldn't just shut down and everybody go hunt the killer. "The work has got to go on." Jake was at the head of the table and his eyes searched the faces of the others. "Before we get started I've got some serious news; Matt, the Marshal from San Antonio sent word, that Tieg feller you captured and took to the Sheriff escaped, all of us are gonna have to watch your back until he's caught. Now let's talk about what needs to be done now that Pa's gone. Some of us have got to keep the place running, and

45

there are the ranch affairs to be settled. We got to settle who's gonna take charge and run the ranch."

Jake held up a paper "This is what pa put down in case something happened. It says the ranch belongs to all of us equally and it told us where he had the money hid. It says to choose one of us to run the place and for everybody to do his part to make the place pay. Near as we know there is about thirty thousand head of cattle, about two thousand broncos and a little over a hundred thousand acres of land.

Jake stopped and cleared his throat, "he left a personal note; I'm going to read it as it's wrote." Boys, I'm passed on or you wouldn't be reading this, I hope you remember me as men should remember their pa. I done my best that's all any man can do. Boys are supposed to have both a pa and a Ma. God took your Ma. I couldn't be both. I taught you what you needed to be a man. I'm proud to say I've raised good men. But there was no one to teach you the nicer side of life and I'd have to say you missed out on the things your Ma would have taught you. Do your best to be the men both of us would be proud of. I ain't one for soft words but I reckon you know how I feel about you.

Jake looked at them with a wry smile. "He signed it pa."

"There's an account book and a bank book because some of what's left is in the bank, and the rest was hid here on the ranch. Let's settle who you want to run the place and who's going to go after the one who shot pa."

Matt stood up, "We know Jake's gotta run this place and there are things that can't be left undone. Let Tucker and me go get the scum that murdered "pa."

"I'm going!" stated Cord. "I don't need anyone's permission, I am flat out going and that's it." Cord was just next to Matt and three years older. He was heavier and slower than Matt but as hard headed as a rock. Once his mind was made up that's the way it was. Jake could see heads nodding in agreement "I think that we'll put off all the other details until these boys have taken care what needs to be done. Let's load them up, the trails getting old."

The Sheriff was on the porch when the Teal's came out. "Jake, we followed that bushwhacker clear to the border where he crossed into Mexico. I ain't got no authority over there. Of course you boys are going after him no matter where he run's too. I brought badges for each of you, I don't know if they'll help any but they might, so take them and keep them hid until ya have a need. Good luck to ya and our prayers go with you." Tucker held out his hand. "Many thanks Sheriff, that's mighty thoughtful of you. We won't forget the backup we got from our friends."

The lawman held out some sheets of paper, "these tell who you are and what your purpose is, it might come in useful."

Tucker passed out the badges and the letters that identified them, shook hands all around and they mounted up.

From the front porch, about two hundred yards away towards the north side of the house there was a wrought iron enclosed area; it had protected their family burial plots for as long as Matt could remember. But now there was a new grave there, Matt looked at it as they rode out, wondering how long it would be before it held some more of their body's. He looked at Cord, but Cord was looking straight ahead, his jaw was clinched. Matt could see the side of his brother's face, it was flushed red and his eyes were wet. He figured this was not the time to speak but he wondered about the tears. He had seen tears in all their eyes; he hadn't shed any tears. Matt hadn't felt the way some of the others had; he didn't feel the emptiness and even the sadness. What he felt was indignation and anger that anyone would dare to harm a member of the Teal family. He was mad clear through. He was killing mad.

They rode straight to the river where the tracks crossed into Mexico. The Sheriff had already tracked the killer that far, but since his jurisdiction stopped there, so had he. They crossed the river, Tucker, Cord, Matt and their pack mules; not knowing or caring how long it would be before they came that way again.

"Cord, you get on up there and pick up on them tracks, Matt you stay back and off to the side so you can cover our back side, you get that Winchester in your hand an keep it ready to fire. I'll ease off to the other side and be where I can keep Cord covered. Let's not make no noise now and keep each other covered." Tucker pulled his horse into the brush.

And that's the way it went. Cord in the lead moving slow, Tucker and Matt shadowing him. Matt was covering Tucker and Cord, and Tucker was covering Cord. It was slow, hot and they were jumpy but there weren't nothing moving not one blamed thing. Not even a breeze to relieve the burdensome heat waves that always shimmered in the distance.

In the middle of the fourth day they had only traveled five or so miles. It takes a lot of time if'n you're following a trail made by a knowing man, Cord had pulled up and swung down from his saddle, and pulled his neckerchief from his neck and wiped his sweaty face.

A shot broke the stillness and Cord was slammed back, and lit hard on the dirt. Matt glanced toward the sound and for just an instant saw a small dark, hatchet faced man running hard to get over a small rise to get out of sight. That image would be one he wouldn't forget. It weren't the clothes, he wore regular range garb, it was that narrow wedged shape face with an overlarge sharp nose and bushy black eyebrows, walrus mustache, and that look that was on it. A look like old Yeller had when it had caught the mouse. And then he was gone and Matt could hear the hoofs of a running horse.

Tucker was down by Cord stuffing Cords neckerchief under his shirt to stop the blood flow. "I didn't see him!" he yelled angrily "Did you get a look at him?"

Matt didn't answer him; he knelt by Cord waiting to see if there was anything to do. Cord opened his eyes for a moment, he had a puzzled look on his face like he couldn't remember where he was, he turned his head towards Matt and his eyes widened in recognition, he smiled and in that brief instant Matt felt something he'd never felt before; kinship and something akin to remorse and sorrow.

"Is he gonna make it?" He asked softly

"He's been hit hard but it didn't hit the heart and it went all the way through if we can get the bleeding stopped he'll make it."

"I got to go," Matt whispered.

"I'll get him; he won't get away."

Tucker nodded his understanding,

"Take the packs, we won't need them. You watch close, he's a back shooter."

"We'll be here awhile." Tucker paused, "Matt we're counting on you, give him some room he'll be wait 'n for a shot at you."

But Matt already knew that and was already on his way. It was the hard driving anger that raged inside him that made him hurry. It was a killing fever. He had an anger inside, he was mad at his pa for letting himself get killed by a back shooter, he was angry at Jake for letting his pa be down by the grave by himself, he was upset with Tucker for exposing Cord to the shooter and he was furious with himself for not seeing the dry gulcher before he could shoot Cord. It wasn't right; there was something bad wrong and Matt just knew that Jake and Tucker had mishandled this whole thing. The anger within was boiling over; if'n it turned out that pa was shot because of something Jake had done he would leave and never come back. In short it was somebody's fault and Matt was as sore as a short tailed bear.

The tracks soon became as familiar as his own hand, the left front shoe was worn to the outside, and the hair caught on the brush was some black and some white. The white was lower down like it was an ankle color. There weren't no other prints so the shooter wasn't using a pack animal. Matt followed those tracks through a small village. Whoever he was he wasn't going to any trouble to keep people from seeing him now. Matt took time to ask if anyone had noticed the rider or the horse. No one had seen the rider or the horse; that was about what Matt had expected. Even though he talked Mex like a native he was still a gringo asking questions of a Mexican. He didn't show the badge, it wouldn't have made any difference. Might of made things worse. Past the village and still headed west he rode watching both the trail and the mesquite and cactus covered hills around him. Today he was not appreciative of the country side, he did not see the pecan trees, nor look at the acres of the blues, reds, and yellow blooms of the beautiful cactus. He did not see the scrub oak intermingled with mesquite and cactus; the beauty of the land along the Rio Grande never crossed his mind. He did find where his quarry had stopped and rolled a cigarette, his horse was turned to face the trail behind him. "So" Matt mused "He's leading me somewhere, probably an ambush."

The tracks cut back north towards the river, cutting through the thick patches of brush and trees until Matt hit another trail. This path was a game and wild cow trail used by only very few human travelers. It was almost parallel to the river now and Matt wondered if he was going to cross back over. It weren't long till that's what happened, he was back on the Texas side again and headed north. But the sun was almost down and Matt knew he was going to have to find a place to hole up. He stepped down to walk awhile, leading his mount he walked slowly watching for tracks. The sun was down; he ate a cold biscuit and jerky and waited till the moon was out. Hot coffee would have tasted good but he weren't ready to show even a small fire. The moon grew higher and brighter and he could read tracks again. Squatting to make sure of his track he glimpsed a light off the trail to the west up a small draw. Standing up he couldn't see it, squatting again he spotted it.

Someone had built a fire and covered it to hide it. But whoever it was hadn't dug a fire pit first, and not figuring on his fire showing he would be less watchful. But when Matt was squatted down looking up the draw it was visible to him. Leaving his horse he put on his moccasins and slipped step by step towards the campfire. He could see a large boulder and figured the fire to be at the base of it. It was a likely spot and it was only by chance that he spotted the fire. He moved slowly and silently.

Suddenly something slammed into him and stumbling he fell. The fall saved his life; he felt the closeness of another bullet as it barely missed his head. He heard the shots as the shooter probed the brush where he lay. He remembered being hit hard, and remembered trying to move. He almost cried out as he fell down the bank to the bottom of a gully. He used his elbows and feet to squirrel under the overhang of the bank into the brush and then nothing. He had no way of knowing how long he was out, but when his eyes opened it was way up in the middle of the day. Matt's head hurt and his shoulder was throbbing with pain, the whole right side of his shirt was covered with blood and blood was still seeping from the wounds. His side was wet, front and back, so the bullet must of went on through. Matt could hear the clop clop of a horse moving up the gully towards him. Hatchet Face was probably searching for his body.

Matt was too weak to stand and there was no place to crawl to. Looking all around, he looked up and wondered if'n he pulled at the weeds on the bank, could he cause enough dirt to slide to cover him. What if he caused more dirt to fall than he could handle? But he could hear the horse moving closer and out of desperation grabbed a-holt of all he could wrap his hands around and pulled hard.

Matt got a little trickle of dirt, so grabbing for more and yanking hard there was a small land slide and he was covered with dirt and rock. He couldn't move or wiggle or even move his legs. The weight was oppressive; he was having a hard time breathing. Desperately he wished he'd of let Hatchet Face shoot him. That would have been better than dying buried alive. Matt grew frantic; he screamed and struggled but was fighting and struggling in vain. The pain was so fierce he blacked out again. Later becoming mindful of where he was at, wished he could have just cashed in without coming back to all this pain.

Matt's body trembled and jerked; he could hear sobbing and knew it was himself. Everything blotted out again and when it seemed like he had come too; it was like he was outside his body looking at himself sobbing, trembling and shaking. He felt a presence; he couldn't turn his head but felt his Pa's hand. Then somehow he could see Pa's face. It was Pa's expression; "If'n you must die son, die like a man, pull yourself together. "Remembering all the times Pa had told him "be a man," There'd never been a word of pity. He'd never seen a tear in Pa's eye. Matt's own inability to feel had been part of his heritage, he realized it but inwardly he shook it off as "too late now."

He could hear thunder in the sky and felt water seeping in around him, so it must be raining. The pain was unbearable and now he was going to be soaked! In desperation Matt cried out "God, I know my Ma believed in you. If you are there would you help me? Would you let me die easy and take this pain away? He had no concept of time; he did not know when one day faded into another. He could hear himself crying and then he would hear himself laughing; a crazy weird out of control laugh. Then he blacked out of it again, barely breathing, not aware of the storm in the hills around him.

A flash flood brought a wall of water, a ripsnorter with waves rolling, boiling, slamming and destroying everything in its path. It came roaring down, vibrating and shaking the ground around Matt, flooding the area, just as it had done time after time for many years. The raging torrent scooped up the little land slide along with him and carried him in waves of debris and rolling water, fighting to stay on top it rolled him under. Tossing, bruising, and slamming him from side to side. Finally, where the banks of the gully made a sharp turn he was causally tossed up on a bank, soaked through and through, bloody and hurt. Matt had so little life left he just laid there.

CHAPTER SIX

As Matt was coming around he could feel a sharp pain in his side, shifting around a little he realized he was a- laying on his knife that was hung around his shoulder by a strap. He instinctively touched his six- gun; it was still in his holster, held there by the thong over the hammer. The other feeling was from a tongue licking his face. There was strong wet dog smells that come with the washing he was getting. He strained to set up, there was really sharp pains, that was made worse by the attempt, and he was hurt 'n bad enough to make him just let go and flop back down. The tongue moved to his hand and he moved his hand to reach the top of the dog's head. The dog whined and scrunched closer to him. Even with him wet and smelly he brought a sense of comfort. His presence drained away some of the frantic desperation that Matt was feeling. He was alive! And he had thought it was all over. He was elated yet his nerves were bound up tight, together they slept away the rest of the day. The dog never moved as though he was afraid, at times his whole wooly body shook with violent trembles, every time he shook he spread the wet dog smell until Matt smelled just like him. With the white dog lying side by side with him, he realized the dog was over six foot long. His body and head was hugh and the animal must weigh about a hundred and fifty pounds or so.

Evening came and the dog stood up; hunger was winning out. He needed a rabbit or a small quarry to eat. He was a very big dog with a very large shaggy head. His legs were long and his teeth were big, no rabbit had ever escaped such big teeth. With his nose he nudged Matt, who came awake, his hand clawing for his gun. When he saw it was a dog, his heart quit pounding so hard. "I thought you was the back shooter," he told the dog. His only answer was eager whines and a large bushy tail wagging.

Matt drifted off again and the next time he came too it was raining. There was nothing to do but hunker down and wait it out. He was so exposed and felt so helpless. The rain clouds had made it so dark the moon didn't shine through and it was so pitch black that he couldn't see a hand in front of his face. But then Hatchet Face wouldn't be able to move around either.

He wondered how Cord was doing; if he was still alive. It had looked pretty bad, but it was hard to tell about bullet wounds. It was a chest wound and that was probably better than one in the gut. Tucker was with Cord and Tucker knew a lot about bullet wounds. He'd learned a lot during the war. He'd dug a lot of Yankee lead outta men and patched them up whilst they waited to get on the hospital wagons. Jake had told it that the men were saying if you were gonna take lead be sure that Tucker was close by you. Jake and Tucker had stayed together through the whole war.

All his brothers were in the war except Cord. Bruiser wouldn't let Cord go, he said he was too young and now

THE TEN DOLLAR ROAD 57

Cord had been shot anyway. Matt wondered if there was a set time to die for every one like some of the cowboys believed. He'd heard it argued that when it was your time to go you'd go no matter what or where. Jake would just laugh; he didn't believe there was a higher plan for everybody. Bruiser said that if there was a higher plan it was based on how well you could take care of yourself. Matt's Ma had believed in God and prayed every day but it hadn't helped when she was being dragged behind that horse. Matt decided that Bruiser was right; you had to take care of yourself. The first time you were careless and weren't watching was when you died.

As the light of day was breaking the rain slowed down and by sunrise it'd quit altogether. Matt made it to his knees and could look around; there weren't much to look at. A bunch of boulders layup by the rim rock that was probably a hundred and fifty feet high and stretched as far as the eye could see. There were about two hundred feet of rough, rocky ground between him and the rim rock. Around the valley was a number of tall cap rock plateaus; some just covered an acre or two, others were much larger. Amongst the brush and the trees at the base of the plateaus were scattered giant rocks and boulders, some of them house sized. And of course the wash-out where he'd been caught in the flash flood. There seemed to have been a heap of things washed up where he'd been tossed out on the bank. Matt finally pushed his-self up; it cost him a lot of effort and he endured a lot pain but he made it to his feet. The bleeding had stopped; his shirt was stiff with dried blood. He was so woozy that he had tiny black spots in his vision and he had trouble with his balance. Forcing his-self to move he stiffly limped over to look through the wet and muddy stuff washed up by the flash flood, he needed to stay alive and there just might be something there that would help.

There were lots of brush, some tree limbs and a lot of mud. He searched a ways downstream without much luck. Turning upstream he found what had been his pack horse lying on its side; but his pack was still there, although he'd have to cut the straps to get it loose because the horse was laying on most of the pack, and he was so weak he couldn't get the straps out from under him. When he'd packed the horse he'd wrapped everything in oil cloth, to keep it dry if'n it rained. Now he spread everything out on the oil cloth. Some of it was a little damp but wrapped like it had been it weren't water damaged. He decided to leave it out under the sun's rays for a few hours. He had to keep shooing the dog back away from the bacon, and that reminded Matt of how long it'd been since he'd had a bite to eat.

He stirred through the pile of stuff and found his sling, gathering a few rocks he snapped his fingers at the dog and said "let's go get dinner." The big dog bounced up quivering, he seemed to be aware of what Matt wanted and took off for the rocks. They found a spring of pure clean water tumbling out of the rocks. The rocks were infested with big fat rabbits. It didn't take long to bring down enough of them to put four over his fire. Whilst the rabbits were hanging over the fire on a limb, he went back to searching through the rubble. He was looking for his Winchester but it was probably covered by the mud, he did find his rope and stretched it out to dry. He kept turning his head and looking for Mouse, he didn't want to lose his saddle and the saddlebags. All the herbs and medicines and salves were someplace in the saddle bags.

Him and Mouse used to play a game of hide-n seek where he would slip off and hide and wait for Mouse to come and find him. Mouse had a nose like a blood hound and always in a few minutes he would find Matt, then he would neigh loudly. He really liked to win. Matt figured Mouse to be searching for him and hoped he'd hurry up and find him. He wanted his saddle bags and the slicker that was tied behind the saddle with his possible bag. He felt bad about the packhorse but was plain ole happy it weren't Mouse.

He came on a little leather case that weren't his. It was some kind of doctor's bags that held a bunch of shiny knives and pliers. There were bottles of stuff he would have to study out latter. There was laudanum in bottles, Matt swallowed a little, he needed just enough to cut the pain to where he could get around without moaning. The dog was still by the fire watching the rabbits and Matt could see they were good and brown so he went back and set them on a rock to cool. The big ol' dog was hardly able to set still and was drooling all over the place.

They ate the rabbits whilst they were still a little hot. One was enough for Matt but the dog ate the other three and nosed around for the bones Matt left. He buried the spot where the fire had been and covered it with some of the rocks.

Hatchet Face was probably still searching for him and he weren't ready for no fight yet. He decided to take one more look in the rubble by the gully. The water was gone on by now and what was left was the things the run off had carried down the gully and had left at the sharp turn where Matt had been tossed up on the bank. There was lots of mud and brush, he took a tree limb and cut the branches off in order to have a usable stick. He used that to poke through the debris. He heard a moan and the brush moved. He jumped back in surprise. He could see an arm; waded in and grabbed it and pulled. It was a man, a small thin man. His head was splattered with blood, he was still breathing but just barely.

Matt ignored his own pain and pulled the feller out of the mud and up on the bank. He was all muddy, soggy wet, and mostly dead. Once he'd cleared away the mud, he found where a gash made a slight furrow alongside his head. The effort of pulling him up on the bank had just about done Matt in; he was too weak and too sore all over to carry the fellow, so he just left him laying where he was.

What was strange was that the dog walked stiff- legged around him and growled low ominous growls, whilst showing his teeth; as though he were ready to tear him apart. Matt had a hard time calling him away from the man. Then because the dog was acting so strange he decided it would be good sense to go through the man's pockets. The only things he found was a money wallet and a derringer hid in a special made pocket. Leaving the money he kept the small gun. It had four barrels and when it fired, it fired all four barrels at once. Since he didn't know the feller he figured he'd hang onto the gun. If'n he woke up and wasn't the agreeable sort it'd be better off in Matt's pocket. If'n he didn't wake up then Matt would deal with the money wallet later. The strangest thing of all was a belt buckle gun. Matt had heard of them but had never seen one. This feller wasn't packing a six- gun where ya could see it, but he had a collection of hide out hard ware. He put the belt buckle gun on and wore it; it might come in handy.

He walked around pulling small limbs from the pile of brush and managed to build a small shelter. He used some of the many rocks around to build a fire pit. He had made it deeper because the bottom was where he built an oven. Over that was the campfire for cooking and heat. Two days had passed and the man still lived but had never stirred.

Whilst Matt waited he rolled some big rocks together for a place to make a stand from; there was not only Hatchet Face but also Indians who probably used this valley as part of their trail north. After thinking about the possibility of being caught out in the open he moved his bedroll further up in the rocks. He'd bed down where he didn't feel so exposed.

He'd found some cat-tail and put a bunch to soak in the water from the spring. Later he would remove the fibers and let the starch settle. He could make fine white flour from it. Over by where the flood had drained away, he'd seen some ground nut and the roots made a good potato substitute. From what he could see around him there was plenty of food. Even the cactus would come in handy. "Me and dog will make out," he mused. "If'n we can stay outta of the way of injuns and Hatchet Face. If only Mouse would find me and bring my rifle." The basics being taken care of he was restless and began to walk further and further out.

He didn't know what brought it to mind but he recollected a story old Sam had told him. It was about a place along the Nueces River where it crossed the old San Antonio to Laredo Road. It was place of vast open spaces, close up to the San Caja and Las Chuzas Mountains. Thousands of acres of land covered with cactus, chaparral, scrub oak, and every thorny bush known to mankind. Ravines, canyons, small hills and deep crevasses cover the area. There was a spring coming out of the rocks and according to old Sam's story just a ways from that spring and about half way down a ravine was the entrance to a large cave. Inside that cave there was supposed to be stored silver and gold; put there by robbers who worked the San Antonio to Laredo road and who also robbed silver from the silver mines of the Spanish.

South and east of the springs was what Matt remembered. The story was told by old Sam who had found the springs and had not realized what they represented until later, and then was never able to find them again. Hidden treasure stories were common in Texas; there were lots of them. But Matt had believed the old man was telling it because he really believed it. He was going to take a look-see anyway.

He checked on the stranger, but he was still out. He hadn't even stirred or turned over or even moved a leg, Matt didn't believe he were going to make it. He had quit bleeding through the nose and ears and it looked like the swelling where the groove was across his head had gone down some, but his breath come in small gasps and in jerks. He did figure the fever was down a little too. The thought crossed his mind that maybe the doctor's bag belonged to this feller.

If'n he would wake up he could fix him some teas from plant's he recognized along the ravine. They were known for reducing fevers and helping with the healing. But he couldn't use them until the man was awake enough to swallow. Anyways he wished the man would either get well or die. He guessed he would have to shoot him if'n he didn't start stirring around; he sure couldn't just walk off and leave him like that.

CHAPTER SEVEN

There just wasn't anything he could do about him right now, so he took off in search of the ravine that Sam had told about in his story. If'n it were there it shouldn't be far away. The problem was that you couldn't tell there was a ravine till you walked up on it, because from a distance all you could see was the roughness of the countryside. Ya had to almost be standing on the lip of it to see it. According to Sam it was supposed to be mostly south from the spring. He decided to set up a compass because the rock walls and the roughness of the place around him were so uneven he might think it was south when it might not be.

He set a stick in the ground and using the leather thong that he used on his sling he measured the distance of the shadow. Where the shadow ended he put another stick then he drew an arc in the dirt. When the sun was high, the shadow shortened and when the sun moved past noon the shadow would get long again. When it grew to where it met the arc again he placed another stick. A line on the arc halfway between the two stakes was south.

It was about where he figured south was but he was enough off that even a little ways out it would of made a pile of difference. The time he took to get his bearings, caused enough delay that the sun had passed overhead. But he decided to start the search anyway. He put his sling back together and called the dog and they started out. He soon found out there was rattlesnakes around. He killed a big bull rattler with his sling and thinking of cutting a couple of steaks from it he started towards it, but the dog beat him to it and was already eating it before Matt could save it. But reminded of the snakes he walked a little more mindful of his steps.

He came on a deep arroyo, hundreds of feet deep with a full stream of rolling, splashing, angry and dangerous wall of water that was falling at a very steep angle into a pool at the bottom. There was a way to climb down; along one side was a faint path strewn with boulders. There was also small rocks, pebbles and some shale that filled the in between low spots. From where he was at he couldn't see anything that looked like a cave entrance, but there did appear to be a fold in the rock wall.

Standing by the fold in the rock was a house sized boulder that had been shaped to the likeness of a human head on a pedestal. It was taller than a grown man but it was egg shaped. There was no telling how long that thing had been there but he had heard that heads like this one had been carved by an ancient people that lived around south Texas and Mexico a long time ago; even thousands of years ago. He stood in wonder at the workmanship and amazed that it could have been carved way back then. What did they have for tools? Why would they spend the kind of time and effort to carve out such a great big head like that? He wondered if'n anybody knew about this head and if'n they did, could they know why?

The dog was making a commotion back up the top so he swung around to go see what the hullabaloo was all about.

There was Mouse and about three other horses calmly lollygagging along, grazing as they walked; the big gray horse saw him and broke into a trot his direction. Matt had never been so happy to see anyone or anything as he was to see Mouse.

The other Cayuses stood and watched as Matt staggered towards them. His saddle, the rifle in its scabbard, along with everything else was still there; whereas the saddle on the black and white paint was dangling by a strap, with everything else missing and covered with blood stains. He remembered the black and white hairs he'd seen on the brush and wondered if'n this was the horse Hatchet Face had been riding.

The other two were pack horses with the packs still attached, though one was a little worse from wear because there had been a determined effort to dislodge it by scraping it against a tree or possibly a rock cliff.

He crawled in the saddle trying to ignore the pain from the hurts he'd suffered. He'd have to finish trying to find treasure some other time. Nudging Mouse back towards where he'd left that feller he'd found in the mud. Hopefully he was either dead or awake. He let the big gray walk along easy and the rest just followed. He wondered how long the critters had traveled like this. It would be helpful to know how far it was back to where he'd been shot.

He had everything from all the packs laid out. He put all the similar things together; but the one pack had nothing he could use. It was full of show business things. Lots of powder, rouge, wigs. There were beards and false ears and even wooden noses. There were funny old timey clothes along with so much stuff he didn't know anything about. That stuff he just rolled up stuffed it back in the bag it came from. But in the rest there was some canned stuff and flour and salt, those things he could use; especially the coffee.

He had his rifle back and in one of the bags from the other pack horses had been a two gun rig complete with pearl handled six guns, plus four boxes of forty fours. He'd always wanted pearl handles; he put that rig on and shifted his own gun to where it fit in the hollow of his back. He wanted to try the guns but being in Indian country he didn't dare for fear the sound of guns would have them injuns in on him like stink on a barn lot.

He cut a couple of poles from the brush pile and tying a blanket between them made a place on it for the wounded feller. Then Matt used one of the pack horses to drag him up to where his camp was. Using the extra bedroll the pack horses had brought in he made the poor feller a little more comfortable by the fire. He got his head up a little higher and poured some laudanum down his throat, just enough so's not to choke him. After that he seemed to rest a bit better.

Matt figured that come morning he was leaving; if'n that feller hadn't come out of it by then he'd just leave him or shoot him, he'd have to decide in the morning. He did get out the man's wallet again and counted his money. He had three hundred and forty five dollars in paper money and eighty dollars in gold coin. Matt figured this man was not an ordinary cow hand. His clothes were too expensive and those boots were special built outta calf leather. What was strange was he weren't wearing a gun belt; in Texas that was unheard of.

The still of the night was interrupted by groans and gasps of pain. Matt could hear the wounded man thrashing around. Instantly Matt was on his feet, but he'd been to slow and had to run to catch him; he was running and screaming whilst holding his head with both hands. It took all the strength Matt could muster to drag him back to the camp; with him kicking and screaming out "that there was billows and rolls of fire attacking his feet" and at the same time he was trying to fight off the devil that was after his soul. Finally after enough laudanum had been forced down his throat, some peace and quiet was restored.

By sunup; the feller was settled down though still in a lot of pain, the rest of that day was spent giving him swallows of teas from a plant with purple flowers and some pulp from the underside of a willow tree bark. The special tea and a poultice that Matt knew would reduce the swelling and take care of the redness around the wound. He was glad he'd spent so much time following Rosa around in the woods whilst she was gathering the right plants for medicine. Rosa had been cook and doctor to the ranch since he'd been just big enough to follow her around.

Matt made him take some broth and drink the special tea with just enough laudanum to let him be able to stand the pain. He wanted to get back to looking for the cave Sam told him about but decided he wouldn't do that until he was all by his own self. Right now he was busy trying to keep things under control at camp. He was busy being doctor and taking care of the stock; seeing to their feed and water. Every day the wounded man was getting better.

CHAPTER EIGHT

There had been campfires to the south last night; this morning there was dust hanging in the air. Matt was hunkered down on top of the rim rock cliff. His eyes trying hard to focus on the dust cloud, it looked like close on to ten mounted men with packhorses. That would make twenty horses or maybe more depending on how much provisions they was toting. There could be a lot of different reasons; they could be a posse, or they could be trail hands going to pick up a herd. Or they might even be outlaws. In any of the cases, it could be trouble. He returned to the campfire; "Ya remember anything yet?" The wounded man seemed discombobulated, "I can't even get my head straight; let alone remember anything."

"Well ya got to have some kind of a handle; I know a feller back home that looks a lot like you, his name is Luther, so I reckon I'll call you after him. From now on I'll call you Luther till ya get your memory back." He got a shoulder shrug "One name's as good as another."

"Well Luther we got trouble coming; there are ten or twelve men headed this way. There're wearing a lot of hardware and packed with enough possibles to last 'em a long time. Could

68

be they're hunt 'n somebody; maybe you, or maybe not you; either way we need to be ready."

"How, we can't fight that many. You're just a boy and I can't even think straight."

"You take the rifle and get up there behind them rocks and I'll face up to 'em down here. Like ya said, I'm just a boy in their eyes and they most likely won't jump on me, at first anyway. If they get froggie with me you can stick that Winchester out where they can see it and they'll probably not be as ready to make trouble as they thought they was."

Matt stood there quietly, with the dog along his side and waited.

They rode up; a rough looking bunch Matt thought. The leader looked like the kind of ranny that was hard shouldered and mean. He was all of that and more; arrogant, tough, and big; he was narrow in-between the eyes and hard eyed. Matt purt near swallowed his teeth, there sat bank robbing Johnny Tieg and he began to feel like he had an upset stomach. He tried to stay calm but inside he knew there was going to be some shoot 'n. And there was a lot more men on their side. The big feller said.

"They call me Smoke; I'm the he coon here. Kid, this here is Injun country; what in blazes ya doing out here?"

Johnny Tieg reined his mount close up by the big man.

"Watch that kid Smoke, he's a back shooter and faster 'n a snake with that shoot 'n iron. He's the one that shot me in the back! Let's fill him full of lead."

Smoke never even turned his head, "shut up! Are you a coward?"

"I'm looking for a bushwhacker that come this way," Matt said.

"Who is it?"

"Don't know his name yet but he's dark skinned, thin and small with a hatchet shaped face and wearing a lot of hair under his nose."

"We might know him boy, half the size of a man and all mean. He's called "Half a Bob" and hangs out around German Town. There's a woman there, Esther somebody. German girl there that wants a man, any man, and he's besotted by her. He's too tough for a boy like you to take on."

"I do thank you mister, I thank you kindly. But he back shot my pa from an ambush and I am going to kill him."

"Who was your pa? Must have been somebody important? Half a Bob only kills for money and a lot of money at that."

"My pa was Bruiser Teal and I'm Matt Teal."

"I've heard tell of you boys, heard you were raised with the bark on; which is good because ya need to be tougher 'n a boot to get Bob. By the way young feller, I need a couple of spare Cayuses I reckon I'll take a couple of yours, ya got four and that's more than you need. I'll take that gulla and that black and white pinto. I'll pay you ten dollars apiece for 'em."

"I don't have any horses to spare" Matt answered.

"I'm taking those two and you're lucky I'm buying them; so don't push me boy."

About that time, they heard a click as Luther cocked his rifle. They could see the rifle barrel as Luther aimed it over the top of the rock. "Well that shows us where one of them fellers is boss, you suppose there's two more? There's four horses, maybe there's three Teals behind them rocks." The rest of his crew was shifting nervously looking all directions.

"Got me euchred have you boy?"

"I reckon so" answered Matt. "A lot of you could die here."

"So could you boy."

"Yeah, but your dead certain to be the first, there's no doubt about that."

He laughed and winked at Matt; "Just fooling, I wanted to see what you were made of; I figure you'll do. Old Half a Bob best be headed out of this country or he'll be planted here. I don't want no gun play or I'd let you have Tieg, maybe you'll run into him later. "Watch your back!"

With that he waved his men on and they left grinning at him whilst some of them gave a wave goodbye.

Luther climbed down from the rocks, "I wonder which way it was? Did he intend to take the horses or was he just testing you."

Matt just shrugged his shoulder, "Surprised him I guess; he thought I'd be scared and he could bully me. Let's pack up and move outta here before they decide to come back."

Luther laughed, "It did me good to see that arrogant would be bad man take water." Matt kind of grinned, nodded his head, and let it ride.

Luther continued, "What did that feller have against you? He sure wanted them to fill you full of lead. You must 'of knew him, huh?"

"He robbed a bank and I took him in. I had to shoot him to stop him he was a-fixing to run. We have to move quickly now, they might come back or them Kickapoo's might show up, we're in their bailiwick and we don't want to be caught here. They might not like us being here!"

"Is this the way to Texas?" Luther asked.

"Yep, the Indians use it, the miners use it, and outlaws use it and we don't want to be found by any of them. The Indians used it a longtime, even before the white man came here."

"I wonder how come nobody has put up a trading post or sump 'em."

Matt answered, "This country is too wild and too dangerous. Those Kickapoo's live in Mexico and use this trail a lot; they are plumb mean and fierce fighters. They wouldn't cotton to the idea of white traders settling on what they figure is theirs. They come over to Texas and raise all kinds of a ruckus, steal everything they can carry and drive off with the cattle; killing and scalping as they go."

"Then how come Texas doesn't do something?"

"Because they run back across the border and Mexico say's we can't go across after them. I hear we're a-going to raid them anyway. My guess is probably pretty soon."

"Well I hope we don't run into anymore outlaws or injuns; this is a really wild country out here."

Matt laughed, "This ain't a place for tenderfoots or sissies."

Luther pondered that for a while, "As soon as I get my memory back I think I'll go find a town to live in. Where we headed anyway?"

"We're headed for German Town. Sam told me when ya don't have a man's trail to follow look for his woman."

They camped that night in a little draw that was hidden by a stand of trees; that not only covered the draw but also angled on up the hill almost to the top. The tree line followed a small winding creek that you could step across at any point. Matt found a couple of downed trees that formed an almost perfect corral and he turned Mouse and the other horses loose. There was grass, water, and space big enough for 'em to roll in. He banked the fire under the heavy tree foliage, to keep the smoke thinned down so as not to give their position away. Luther unrolled their blankets and set up camp. The dog scouted the area for a rabbit, whilst Matt made pan biscuits and coffee gravy. Of course, the gravy wasn't as good as gravy at home but on the trail, it weren't bad. The coffee was good. Maybe tomorrow they'd get close enough to a prairie hen or two that Matt could use his sling. They couldn't use their guns because they were traveling through injun country. If'n it weren't the Kickapoo's it would be the Comanche's they were both bad news.

Matt had it in his head that Hatchet Face would probably head for German Town. He'd know that the heavy rain had blotted out all his tracks and there would be no way for anyone to follow him. Figuring that he was safe he'd most likely head for home, if'n that was where he lived and if'n the woman he courted lived there.

CHAPTER NINE

The small band of Apache's had been following the little wagon train for three days now. They were mostly young boys who had decided to follow Yudhajit. Yudhajit was a war chief in his tribe; he was in his early thirty's and very cautious. The young men wanted scalps and a victory, and were pushing him to attack; but he would not be pushed. He had a small band of fifteen young warriors with bows and arrows; the wagon train had that many grown men with rifles. He needed an advantage and would wait until he had one. If nothing happened, they would steal as many horses as they could manage and run.

One of his young warriors had spotted two mounted men headed in the general direction of the wagon train, and there was three eager scouts trailing them. They might be easy scalps to take, and their scalps would quiet the complaints for a while. He was very tired of young warriors finding fault with him; they did not do this to his face, of course, but he was aware of scornful contemptuous terms like "old woman" being used against him behind his back. If they had dared to say such things to his face, he would have sent them on their way back to camp to work with the woman. He had not let on he knew these things yet; he remembered the impatience of the young. While he was thinking on these things, he noticed the young girls that walked behind the last wagon, playing little girl games, giggling, trying to get the attention of the boys. He had seen them before but he just now realized how useful they might be. They might be able to capture one of them and that would give his warriors something else to do and help put an end to the complaints. He smiled as he thought of the scouts he'd sent to keep track of the two horsemen they'd found. They were the eager ones; and the one's most critical of him; and they might disobey his orders to do nothing but watch. If they did, they would regret it.

The wagons below him were circling. They always brought the horses they rode into the circle; the woman and children always remained inside the protected area. Except when they relieved themselves, even then they took armed guards with them. Except one, there was one who slipped away just outside the camp lights and squatted by herself. They might try for her tonight. She was very pretty and was a woman of sixteen years or so. She had plainly said she would not have men gawking at her in her nightclothes while she did what she had to do. She had screamed it at the wagon master. He had spread his hands in a helpless jester and walked away. The chief reflected that Indian girls did not talk back to chiefs and would have no such modesty. She would pay for that disobedience; tonight might be the time.

Two of his warriors come riding hard towards camp; it was too hot a day to be pushing their ponies that hard and he went to meet them planning to speak to them about saving the strength of their mounts for the time they really needed them.

They were supposed to be hunting and he could see no game; anger began to form in his mind against them. They came off their ponies running towards him before their mustangs had even stopped. The ponies sides were heaving and their bodies were lathered in sweat, they tried to catch their breath. Yuidhajit shook his fists at them angrily.

"I should beat you," He thundered "Have you not become men yet? I will send you back to the women to be nursed some more."

"But Chief Yuidhajit we have important things to tell you." Yuma burst out excitedly. "We have seen many men headed this way." Holding out all ten fingers towards his Chief, he was fairly bouncing with excitement; Yuma continued. "They have many horses loaded with packs and they have many guns; and their packs are full. We left Yuyutsu to follow them and have hurried straight to you."

"Did you think they would disappear or be swallowed up in the earth? Is there some reason you have acted like little children that you should abuse your ponies so?"

Both boys stood chastised; they had thought to be bearers of big news and to be praised, not to be scolded in front of the others.

Nevertheless, their Chief wanted all the young men to learn from this lesson. He had trained many young warriors and this was his mission now, to give them experience and guidance at the same time.

"It is not a warrior's way to run about like a crazy man; what you have seen is very important and that you came straight to me was right. You had time to ride back here without using up your ponies. A warrior would have considered the need and acted in a warrior's manner. We will let them camp and then we will take their scalps."

That announcement brought much excitement but no yelling or cheers, because the chief had already been very explicit about noise. "Make ready your arrows; let not one of you be short of arrows tonight. All knives must be sharp and you get some sleep now so that you are well rested and ready."

The scouts that were watching Matt and Luther rode in and gave their opinion that the two men with the pack animals were easy prey. War Chief Yudhajit thought that maybe if all went well they could do both. To that end, he sent one scout back to watch the two riders and told the others to rest.

The campfire of the ten men was well placed and the fire was not big meaning these were not greenhorns. The war chief placed his men in a semi-circle in the darkness facing the camp patiently waiting until all eight were asleep; which left the night watch guarding the horses and another guard who watched over the camp. It was sunrise when he gave the signal; the war cries were loud and the arrows flew. It was a total surprise. The first to die were the sleepy guards; and there were four more dead by the fire, leaving only the four that managed to escape; Smoke, Tieg and two others. They were on foot. They were together and Yudhajit judged that those four who still had their rifles and six guns were too dangerous to follow. Also, it had taken too long to get the captured horses and all of their captured supplies together. The sun was well up and good judgment dictated they should get back to the main camp. Matt and Luther were not going to be pursued this day.

The sounds of the attack had been heard by Matt and Luther. They pulled up, and let their horses rest a spell.

"Reckon some folks are down. That was a short battle. Not very many shots were fired," observed Luther. Matt swung down outta his saddle, "Maybe we better wait here a spell."

"Maybe it was the Injuns that got the worst of it," suggested Luther.

"Maybe," agreed Matt, "but I figure it were the other way around."

The dog was running over by the crown of the hill and he stopped and stiffened with a low bass growl; the one he used when he was seriously perturbed. Matt walked over to him; down below in the lower hills several miles away; he could see four men walking. It figured they would be staying off the hilltops and the top of the ridges was Matt's judgment. Luther had walked up beside him.

"That's them fellers we had the run in with. I wonder where the rest of'm are?"

"Dead;" Matt's voice had a hard edge to it.

"I don't think we ought to go down there." Luther told Matt, "I know they need help but they'd just try to kill us for our supplies and our horses."

"I reckon your plumb right," Matt, answered. "I see Tieg down there. We'll just mind our own business and keep going the way we're headed. But we need to be watching close because there are still those Injuns out there that attacked them."

"We've got dog on our side, he'll warn us." laughed Luther.

"Don't take him lightly," warned Matt. "He will do just that. He's the best dog in this part of the country."

"I wonder where he came from."

"He came with that same gully washer that got us; I reckon he was camped with someone and got caught in the flood."

"Well he sure adopted you; he didn't even try to go find his family; did he?"

"I don't know that for sure, I don't know how long I laid there. It might have been several days. He might have known that they were dead. He found me and stayed; and I'm glad he did."

They stood and watched the big dog as he was watching the four men walking down the hill about a couple of miles away. Then suddenly he turned and crouched almost hiding in the tall grass.

"We got company," Luther said as they mounted; "he's in those tall bushes over there." He pointed towards a clump of high grass and some tall bushes but Matt already had Mouse in an all-out run. Luther had spread a few yards to his right and they both were running their horses hard.

The Indian scout panicked and jumped up from his hiding place; he kicked his pony up from where he had it laying and with a flying leap was on top. He bent over the neck of his bay horse trying not to make a target and was riding for his life. Then the young brave slid around until he was hanging onto the underneath side and stuck to the belly of his bay horse like a flea stuck to a dog. Matt snapped a shot at the bay and it died in mid step. It stumbled and went down right on top of the young warrior. The last thing most cowboys would do is shoot a horse; in fact, most would not 'of shot the pony and because of that; the young warrior would have ridden off.

"We'll leave him just like that," Matt snapped when he saw Luther about to go see about him. "He's probably got a knife in his hand hoping you'll get close enough to stab you in the belly."

"What if he's just hurt?"

"He was here to kill you!"

"Yeah, well there is that, I guess." Luther admitted as he followed Matt.

Slow and careful was their pace. This was where the Apaches raided and you might find them anywhere. Not only Apaches, here were outlaws, renegades and rustlers. It was the kind of country where a man needs to be extra careful. Matt spotted the small wagon train with white canvas stretched tightly over wooden frames. Slowly he moved the glass from front to the tail end of the wagons; he then examined the small herd of mules and horses behind the train. He figured at the most, there were about twenty men if he counted the bigger boys as men. There looked to be a lot of little kids running and playing alongside and even lagging behind the wagons. Probably six or thereabouts families; "they need to get them kids where they can protect them better." observed Matt, "there looks to be a girl about sixteen keeping track of all those kids. They act like there's no danger at all; letting them kids run loose like that." Matt continued. "Let's go by and make sure they know about the injuns stirring around out here."

Luther took a turn with the glass and smiled, "it wouldn't have anything to do with that girl in the blue dress, would it?"

Matt grinned, "Was there a girl in a blue dress? I must of missed her."

"If you missed seeing that girl, you really got eye problems."

Matt turned Mouse towards the wagons and nudged him into a trot. However, Luther kicked his Paint into a run and by the time, they got to the strung out wagons they were in a full-fledged horse race. Mouse was ahead by a full length and Matt ran him by the wagons to give him space to pull up.

They had sure enough made an impression on the folks, some who had seen the race and had been hollering for their favorite. Matt did notice the young lady in the blue dress, he had fastened his glass on, and she had been rooting for Mouse. A couple of the older men walked their direction; the one-stepping out in the lead, appeared to be the wagon master, he was laughing like he enjoyed the race.

"You boys just having some fun or was ya in a hurry?"

Matt dismounted and reached for the offered hand. "There's a bunch of Apache's close by. This morning they killed about six hard men loaded down with rifles and six guns. So they have weapons now to equal yours. You can expect a well-armed attack; most likely in the morning. Their little victory will give them a lot more confidence now."

"Where do you think they are now?" asked the wagon master.

"They most likely took their loot back to their main camp; then they'll strut and crow for the women's benefit. They'll tell everybody what big warriors they are, drink whatever whisky they found and sleep till morning then come and attack you."

The wagon master and the men around him stood mulling it over.

"Are we close to some place like a big ranch or maybe a town where we can head to for safety?"

"There' a town north of here but you won't make it in a day. You best find a good place to circle up and defend yourselves." The wagon train folks had all gathered round; including the girl in the blue dress, Matt was sure she was the best looking of all the girls there. He saw her giggling with one of the other girls but noticed that her eyes were fixed on him.

"We'll go on a-ways," the wagon master said. "We've got to have a spot where we have water and we really need some kind of place where we have protection on a couple of sides so we don't have to defend all four sides."

"There's wagon sized rocks to the west right close to a fair sized pond that we saw coming in," Matt said. "If'n ya could get between them, the pond would block off one direction and the rocks would block two ways so they would only be able to come at you from one direction."

"How far?"

"About two hours for the wagons I'd judge."

The wagon boss stuck out his hand, "I'm J.T. to most folks."

"And I'm Matt Teal and that good looking feller is called Luther."

"Well he is sure enough a nice looking rascal," J.T. observed. Then he reared back and hollered! "Ah reckon we'd best lock up the girls."

CHAPTER TEN

There was some more laughter and introductory hand shaking went on during which Matt was introduced to Imogene, the girl of the blue dress, she smiled at him and took a hold of his arm whilst the rest of the introductions were being carried out. Everybody noticed; and there were lots of knowing smiles, except for a couple of the boys who weren't smiling, they took an instant dislike to Matt. The farm boys knew they had a problem; but didn't know what to do because that cowboy wore a gun and looked plenty tough. Matt was really enjoying Imogene's company, it only lasted a short while till her momma called her back to their wagon and from the look on momma's face, she wouldn't be coming back out that night. Luther had spent time with the men and found out where they came from and where they were going, and the entire whys and wherefores. They rolled their bedrolls next to one of the wagons; not Imogene's, and whilst the fires were dying, Luther brought Matt up "to snuff" on all the things he'd found out. Luther finally drifted off to sleep but Matt's head was whirling with too many thoughts for him to sleep, he'd never had a girl show interest in him before and he was too excited to rest. His head whirled with thoughts and imaginations and sleep didn't come until almost daylight, and then he slept, for almost two hours. Luther woke him and he really didn't want to get up; but they were getting the wagon train ready to move and he didn't want to appear lazy.

They never fixed any fires or cooked for breakfast as J.T. wanted to take no chances of being caught out in the open. So by first light the wagons were rolling. Matt and Luther were leading off since they knew the way. It was a mighty quite bunch that they were leading. There weren't any laughing or noise of any kind; even the little ones seemed to understand the seriousness of their situation. The men trudged alongside the wagons toting their loaded weapons with them; all eyes were peeled watching the brush and such for any sign of enemies. The mood was somber and faces were grim.

They pulled into the chosen spot in good time using only two hours to get there. The men went right to work filling the in between places of the rocks with whatever trees they could cut down; they piled up large rocks to back up the timber they used and in short order they were as secure as they could make it.

Cook fires, coffee boiling and food cooking lightened the mood. Matt sat on a rock and idly watched Luther play with that black and white paint horse that had followed Mouse into their camp. First Luther would chase the paint and then the horse would run at Luther. They were having fun and Matt laughed at some of the antics of the pair as they played. Funny how quick they hit it off, Matt mused. Or was it so quick? Could Luther be the real owner of that horse and not remember it? And if he was; could he be the shooter? Maybe that feller was wrong about who the shooter was or maybe he was just laying a story on them. It could be there weren't any such feller as Half a Bob. It was the horse the shooter had used; that much Matt knew by looking at the horse's tracks. The left front shoe was worn to the outside and the white hair was on the lower part of the leg. He'd know those tracks anywhere after following them for days. But he'd been figuring Luther and that doctors case kind of went together, and he weren't ready to see him as the shooter yet.

Luther didn't seem like he could be a hired killer; but then what do hired killers look like? If'n he put on one of those fake wooden noses and wore one of those mustaches that were in with that theater stuff, would he look the part? Matt's nerves tightened up; he didn't want Luther to be the one. What would happen if'n Luther got his memory back? Would he run or would he come after Matt? Matt decided to watch Luther real close from here on out. That night after the lookouts had been set and folks were in bed he asked Luther if his memory had come back any at all.

"No," answered Luther. "Matt what if I was a bank robber or somethi'n? What if I'm wanted by the law?"

Matt laughed, "Luther you're just not cut out to be like that." And in his thoughts he hoped that was really so.

Chief Yudhajit and Yuma were lying in the tall prairie grass watching and mapping a war plan.

"I think it would cost many braves to attack and very little chance of winning," the Chief said. Quietly they slipped away. Later he spoke with his young braves, "We will keep track of them; somewhere they will make a mistake and we will still have much to carry away. Many guns, much food and horses and mules and we will have many of their women."

The wagons stayed put and on alert for two days until the wagon scouts reported no Injun sign within a day's ride from any direction. It weren't any surprise to Matt that Luther decided to stay with the wagons. He was plumb taken with Imogene and she was a natural born flirt. Matt could see she was keeping all the boys in a dither whereas Luther could only see the calf eyes she was making at him. There weren't no way to get Luther to see the truth and he wouldn't thank a man for trying; he already was showing signs of jealousy whenever Matt spoke to her. So Matt left him the black and white horse, the soogan and half of the possibles they had, including every bit of the stage stuff; the makeup and wigs and such that he said he wanted. He gave him the six-gun he had brought from home and kept the pearl handled forty fours he had coveted. He felt a little bit guilty about that because they really weren't his either; but he rationalized it by telling himself that Luther couldn't use them the right way anyhow. There was no way he was going to give back the derringer or the belt buckle gun; he'd been carrying them ever since he'd took them off of Luther because he saw how sometime it might be the difference between living and dying.

They'd been riding a-while when Matt looked down at the dog that had been trotting alongside of Mouse all morning; "I'm going to give you a name, I'm going to call you King; it's got to be King because you are the best of all the dogs I've ever been around."

The newly designated King, knowing Matt was talking to him, smiled. The lips pulled back into an actual grin because he liked being talked too. And in a couple of days he answered to the name "King" as though he'd always answered to that name.

"Maybe I hit on your real name," Matt told him and King just wagged his tail and grinned some more.

German Town was west and north and he reckoned it was about three days away. His mind drifted back to the ranch and he wished he knew about Cord. One good thing was the bullet hadn't hit anything like a lung or the heart and he had Tucker to look after him.

He knew the boys were still putting together a herd and the work was still going on. They would know that he wouldn't quit and someday he'd bring that varmint back to the ranch to be hung.

Mouse ambled along picking the easy way through the ankle deep cactus and weeds, avoiding rocks and being careful where he stepped on the uneven ground. Then Matt spotted a trail a ways over to the north of him that appeared to be headed the same direction he was headed. It weren't a wide well used trail but it was better than riding across the prairie through the patches of cactus and brush with stickers and thorns. Mouse picked up the pace a little and Matt let him pick the gait that he was comfortable with.

CHAPTER ELEVEN

Matt sat in his saddle and stared; right in the trail was a bad hurt injun. He could see at least two gunshot holes and there was blood all over the front of him. His first thought was to ride on around him or maybe finish him off. He needed to get on up the road and didn't have the time for this, but the red man stirred and moaned; he still lived! King whined and licked the man's face, like he liked him. Matt frowned; he didn't need the interruption and there wasn't a lot of daylight left. He swung down from Mouse and knelt down by him; careful just in case the injun had a knife, but there weren't no weapons showing. His black eyes stared at Matt.

"Me Kickapoo, when you kill me you get to be big man."

With that, he seemed to gather together all of his dignity and cloth himself with stoicism. He weren't gonna tuck his tail in, eat crow or plead for his life. Matt decided he would help him if'n he could. With a small campfire going and the Indian bandaged as best he could Matt settled back to wait. The dog laid down between him and the Indian, his head resting on his paws; that instinctive trust of the animal plus the warmth of the fire, and as tired as he was; he went to sleep. The sun was pretty high when he opened his eyes; startled at having been asleep his first thought was for his horses and his gear. The Kickapoo lay there watching him.

"No one come, I would have woke you."

Matt nodded, "Thanks, who did this to you?"

"A white rancher who has many horses, he did not want me to take his horse." He grinned at Matt, "He leave horse in pasture like him no want; so I take."

"You best be faster or give up stealing horses" advised Matt un-concerned about the attempted theft. "I'm going to leave ya some medicine and bandages. You should be all right now; there's some bacon and coffee, flour and such to last ya a few days."

"Why you do this? I'm Kickapoo, I'm no friend."

"I like the brave way you face me, and I really don't know why except I just feel like doing it."

The Kickapoo closed his fist and thumped his chest in some kind of salute. "Because you warrior too."

Matt liked the injun, he especially liked the roguish glint in his eyes, injun he might be, but Matt figured he was a man to be reckoned with as well.

Matt rode away with the big dog trotting alongside of him. He liked the way the injun had said "you warrior too". He figured Jake would have just shot the red man and rode on not even giving him another thought. Matt was beginning to think that not all the ways he'd been taught was the only way to act, like the killing of the nester. In his mind, going back over that night, it might have been just as well to help them settlers get on down the road. They weren't looking to roost around Two Track. It might have been that the boys just wanted to hurrah somebody. He felt a little guilty thinking like that; was he a turncoat to his own folks by not agreeing with them? But that old nester meant something to them people just like his pa meant a lot to him. He'd give anything to have his pa back.

Why would anyone ambush his pa?

Who would be such a coward that he would kill pa that way? Could it be like Tucker had said that someone had paid a hired killer? If that were so, who would that person be? He felt uneasy in his mind;, there was something he was missing; it was right there in his head but he couldn't get the gist of it. The upshot of it was it nagged at him all the time, there it was, just in the front of his mind but he couldn't pull that thought out.

Who had reason to hate Bruiser that much? He couldn't think of anyone Bruiser had harmed unless it were them hay-shakers when they'd killed that old man. It was either them or someone like them who had received similar treatment. But where would they find someone to do their shooting for them? Not many would want to bring the Teals after them. So Hatchet Face must be new to the country. So was the homesteaders, they didn't know just how bad things were going to get. They'd have a lot better idea when they were all strung up in a row with ropes around their necks! Now he knew he would find them, all of them, Hatchet Face and whoever hired him.

He was looking for newcomers and that narrowed it down a lot; he would find them. German Town was a good place to start. First he would just watch because most likely that would be where the shooter would hang out. As pa used to say" Birds of a feather flock together" and Ma would follow that up with

"Yes and water seeks its own level" and pa would always laugh and say "yer Ma al-ways gets the last word." Matt could see it in his mind's eye; they were saying what they said every time and Matt wished it was like that again and for the first time since his pa died. Matt cried.

He didn't know what he was getting into lately, first he helped that injun and now tears were running down his cheeks. He hadn't cried since he were eleven years old when Ma died and his pa had told him only women cried, men acted and did things to mend the situation but men didn't cry. Of course, there had been tears back there when he'd been stuck under all that dirt but that didn't count. Anybody would've if'n they were buried to where they couldn't even wiggle and death wouldn't come, like it was holding back and tormenting its victim. Just thinking about being buried alive made him shiver with horror and the panic caused his breath to come in spasmodic gulps. He remembered calling out to God for help and wondered if it was God who delivered him. He knew Jake would say it was an act of nature but Jake wasn't always right, and on impulse he raised his head up towards heaven and said, "Sir, I don't know if'n you did it or not but if ya did, I sure do want to thank you." It was a puzzle he decided, how did you know? It was nothing he could figure out right now and he figured to let it go for a while. He could see the buildings of German Town, he knew there was a good chance that there was danger there and could feel the apprehension.

German Town had a sign that proclaimed there were seven hundred and forty folks that lived there. The main road was populated on both sides with small flat board buildings. There was the usual livery stable and barn on the outskirts coupled with a black smith shop. Both buildings were built with unpainted boards. There were four taverns, two general stores, where ya could buy anything from saddles to suits.

There was a boarding house that faced the main road and it housed a café that took up a part of the main floor. Facing the cafe from across the street was a gunsmith's shop and next to that was a saddle maker whose sign proclaimed he was a master craftsman in leather; from leather coats to wallets. On the other side of the gunsmith was the apothecary combined with the doctor's office. Other places along the street were a dressmaker and a stagecoach stop with a barn and corral. All these places looked to be busy.

There were lots of folks moving around, it was being said that there had been a silver strike and men were hurrying gathering up supplies and pack animals. There was some good up standing solid men caught up in the frenzy of instant wealth but there were also thieves, con men, outlaws and those who would scheme and betray others to gain what the good folks had. Matt stood back out of the way for a while and watched the goings on. His first stop was at the boarding house where he paid two dollars and fifty cents for a week's room rent; his dog was twenty-five cents extra. The room was clean and the first time he'd had a real bed in a long time. At the restaurant, steak, eggs, and biscuits covered with gravy was another twenty-five cents. King laid by his feet the whole time and the lady that ran the place gave him a big bone with lots of meat still hanging on it. He gnawed on that bone and thumped his tail a lot. A feller setting at another table growled, "I don't fancy eating with a blamed cur; you put that mutt outside and ya do it now, or I'll kill him."

Matt's ire rose up at the tone of his voice. "Ya better rethink what you're saying; your about to get yourself tangled in your own words."

"Kid you mess with me and I'll put a boot in your bottom."

"Auggie that's a Teal boy," one of his table partners told him. "Leave him alone, Jake's his big brother."

Auggie looked startled. "Aw forget it kid, I just don't like dogs."

King had been staring at him and suddenly he growled a low throaty mean sound.

"I think ya just made an enemy of my dog," Matt said. "He understands most everything ya might say."

Auggie stood up; threw his fork down and stomped out, slamming the door behind him. "It's alright," the cook said. "I'd rather have your dog here than him anytime."

Matt turned to the cowboy who'd told Auggie who he was.

"How'd ya know who I am?"

"I worked for your people a couple of years ago during a roundup. Auggie's a top hand and I didn't want to see him get in bad with your folks. Besides that hound doesn't belong at the table when we're eating; he can wait for you outside the door."

"I'll back you up on that," another hand put in, "We don't cotton to eating with dogs."

King got up; stretched and walked over to the screen door and nosed it open. With a disgruntled grunt, he stretched full length from one side of the stoop to the other. It seemed clear he intended to stay right there and those leaving could jump over him or go out the back door.

"I like your dog," the cook said "but I can't let him run my trade off. You'll have to tie him out back from now on."

"He's like a small kid." Matt explained, "He understands most of what you say and has the same feelings a small pouty boy would have."

The back door slammed as two men left and that was the way the others left. There came another feller wanting in, but not wanting to step over King; he just stood there. Matt left the rest of his coffee to go take King somewhere else. The big dog moved at Matt's "Let's go" but he grumbled as he did, turned, and gave the feller waiting a low-pitched snarl.

The cowboy grinned, "Hey boy; I'm sorry, I didn't go ta make you mad at me."

Matt laughed, "He got his feelings hurt in there and he's taking it out on you."

They went on back to their rented room; Matt set on the front porch, whilst King was asleep, all stretched out under the shade of a big cottonwood tree. Between his front legs, he'd placed a big old deer bone he had picked up along the way. A little neighbor dog snuck up and stole King's bone and King was too slow to catch him. Matt laughed and that laugh was one straw too many; King turned his back to him and three days later still carried a grudge. He wouldn't even acknowledge Matt was there; did not answer a whistle or a finger snaps. Matt did not exist and the big dog would not look in his direction. But the little dog kept on stealing his bones; and he was to slow to catch him. This happened three days in a row and Matt was watching to see how King was going to handle it.

It rained that morning, a real gully washer, and the wagon wheel rut in front of the house was filled with water, Matt was setting on the front steps enjoying the sun shine after the storm. King had a bone lying in front of him and was pretending sleep; Matt was watching, he figured something was about to happen. Sure enough the small thief come a tippy toeing up to grab Kings bone. Then King was on him quicker than a fly on barn yard leavings. He took him by the nape of his neck and lifted him; whilst the little dog was kicking and snarling, he walked him over to the puddle of water and stuck his head under water. Well there was squirming, and jerking and whining and if'n Matt hadn't stopped him he'd a-drowned that little rascal. That was the first good laugh Matt had enjoyed since his pa had been killed. The upshot of it was the little dog never came back and would cross the road to keep from walking by King. For most days, Matt just hung around the livery stables and watched the road. From where he watched, he could see the general store, the three taverns, and the livery.

A few town people and some farmers were moving around one of the saloons. He guessed that one of the other saloons was where the cowboys gathered when they come to town. The other tavern was on the edge of town and was where a red light shined. Heading over to where the range hands gathered he buttoned his coat back away from his guns and pushed the bat wings open and walked in, not really expecting to find Hatchet Face in there but figuring on him eventually showing up. The place had a low plank ceiling, the floor was just boards, and they were dirty and badly stained from spilled whisky and spit tobacco stains. There was only one small window at each end so additional light was provided by two lanterns. The bar was made up of a couple of planks stretched over two kegs. The bad smell was whiskey, sweat and dirty clothes, cleanliness didn't seem to be one of main things on their minds. There were some smirks and nudges up and down the bar probably because he was just a kid, and Matt knew there'd be at least one of them who would have to say something about him being a young'un. He stood just inside the door looking around and mentally sorting and sifting what he could see about each one. Finally stepping on in, he made for the bar. There was a large feller eyeing him who had a cast to his right eye where it had suffered a knife cut; the same knife had gave an ugly twist to his mouth; his mean beady little black eyes followed him all the way across the floor to the bar.

Matt kept his gun hand clear and as he laid his left hand on the bar and ordered a cup of coffee, he was half turned towards the hombre with the glare.

"Hey kid," The one with the cast eye growled, "Ya lost? We don't cotton to little boys in here. So get on outta here, because I don't like you." Matt's hand was a blur but the boom was the sound of a forty-four and the breeze old cast eye felt was of a slug blowing his hat off.

Matt's calm voice broke the astonished silence, "I don't like you, so either go for that gun or get out." They didn't know him but the fast draw and the accuracy was being admired in whispers all over the bar. The problem was old cast eye had spent several hours regaling every one that would listen the supposed history of his many gun fights; and how even

John Hardin, Curly Brocus, and Long Haired Bill, wouldn't face him.

Now this fast kid had called him, he wished he'd just kept his mouth shut; there was no way he could walk out now. "Ya planning on holding that gun on me boy, ya need a head start again old Ned here?"

Matt slipped his Colt back into its holster and stared at Ned, while Ned pulled a cigar out and struck a match to light it. Matt knew that trick and smiled while he waited. The match burned down to where it touched Ned's hand, he swore and tossed the match expecting Matt's eyes to follow the match; but Matt instantly drew and fired. The impact of Matt's slug knocked Ned to the floor, he'd been hit in the shoulder; but Matt had shot to kill. Suddenly he realized that he had been watching for the shoulder to move and he had hit where his eyes had been fastened, he had just re- learned a lesson that he had already been taught by his pa; this lesson he wouldn't forget. "Ya hit what you're looking at." His pa had drilled that into him, now it had been reinforced. Matt pushed his spent shell out and reloaded whilst watching Ned.

"Ya think I look any better to ya now?" That query brought a lot of uproarious laughter and took the tenseness out of the room. Ned looked at his six-gun laying across the floor by the wall; and knowing everyone was laughing at him, he ground his teeth hard and turned and stalked outta the bar; holding a hand against his bleeding shoulder. Everybody else was laughing and carrying on so loud they didn't pay no attention to Ned's retreat. But Matt knew he'd left alive a real enemy that would kill him at first opportunity.

After all the hand pats on his shoulder was done and he'd turned down the many offered drinks, Matt started looking for a way to get back out of the crowd. He felt King brush against his leg, reached down, and petted him. The bartender asked, "Who does that big dog belong to?" Matt grinned. "He's mine; there ain't any way of making him stay outside, he'd just tear the door off and come in anyway."

The bar man leaned over the makeshift bar. "That's the biggest dog I have ever seen in my entire life. Does he bite?"

"Not unless he's being bothered."

"Does he play poker?" one of the card players yelled from the table he was set 'n at.

"No but I do, if'n there's room."

Matt moved over to the table and took a chair, the dog lay down at his feet; with his long white body stretched out, he completely blocked the isle by the table.

A couple of the players reached down and petted him and much to Matt's surprise he just reached out and licked their hands being real friendly. They all agreed he was a real handsome animal. Whilst that was going on Matt realized what an advantage he was. Because of the dog, everybody warmed right up to him and he was accepted right off. He didn't start out asking questions about Hatchet Face he figured on waiting until he had made friends. He played close to his vest; he didn't make big bets and mostly watched the players for a while. He'd learned a lot about playing cards at the bunkhouse from about age twelve.

Sam, amongst the other things he'd taught; had taught him a bunch about poker. Sam had been a professional card player before he'd had his hands buckle up from arthritis. He showed Matt all he knew about cards and card players till Matt could hold his own at the bunkhouse games, and some of them older hands were pert near professionals. He lost a few and won a few of smaller hands, enough to stay in the game. He weren't there to win money but to make friends. So when the pots got expensive he dropped out. Loosing pot money was better than getting involved in the big money. If anybody noticed he was holding back, nothing was said. Besides someone had marked the face cards. He didn't want to make an issue out of the marked cards' because when you called a cheater there was always somebody died. He wanted it to be friendly with no problems he was just after information. Later Matt told his story about why he was looking for Hatchet Face. The men around, all agreed they'd keep an eye out for that back shooter. The name, "Half-a-Bob" didn't bring any information; yet Matt was watching their eyes and saw a few eyes flicker when he brought up his name. These looked like honest cowboys and they probably were but they must not of wanted to be the one to talk about the back-shooter. Maybe Half-a-Bob was so dangerous they didn't want to be the one who pointed him out. Nevertheless, Matt figured even if no-body talked about the short man that his size would give him away.

CHAPTER TWELVE

The big thing that happened that day was Tucker come riding in, Matt had never been so happy to see anybody in his life. He'd needed help but he'd a-died before he would have wired home and asked for it. Of course, Tucker didn't let on he thought Matt might need help; he just came because he wanted away from the ranch for a little while. First thing Matt asked was about his brother Cord.

"Cord's gonna make it; he'll be laid up a-while. I figure one lung got nicked a little but it'll heal with time. Keeping him in bed is the hardest part."

"I reckon that's right, he's a go-er, that's for sure." Matt grinned at the thought of his brother Cord chafing at the bit, ready to go.

They set in Matt's room and before Matt knew it, Tucker had drug the whole story outta Matt.

While they talked, Matt all of a sudden thought about Tucker being there.

"How'd ya know to come here Tucker?"

"The Marshall here wired the ranch to see if you were who you said you was. Said ya pulled a gun over in the saloon on some feller and shot him over nothing. He wanted somebody in the family to come and get you away from here; said you were too good with that gun and too ready to use it."

"That feller picked on me; I didn't jump on him till he threatened me." And then Matt told him how it come about and what happened.

Tucker nodded his head up and down indicating he understood. "Still you got somebody that will kill you first good opportunity he gets. Sometimes you don't use good sense; some of it is your age, but at the same time you're a man now, if Pa were here he'd be plumb disappointed in you."

"I reckon that's so," agreed Matt "but it's over and done with now."

"Not really." Tucker said "I think you need to know where that fellers at all the time, if he's anywhere around you he will make a try for you one of these days when he's got an advantage."

"I think he's left; he'd been telling how bad he was and he left himself with a bronc he couldn't ride. He's lit out for somewhere else where folks haven't heard about what happened."

"Just the same, you be on your guard. Now ya got to watch for two that's after you."

"Two, who else is want 'n my hide?"

"That bank robber, he escaped."

"I knew about him, I met up with him when I met them riders I was telling ya about. He was riding with them. I'll be watching," he promised. "I'm watching everybody right now. I'm wait 'n till Hatchet Face shows up. They call him "Half a Bob" and he's supposed to hang out around here. Which means, he will go to his friends here so they will hide him. He'll show one of these days and I will get a rope on him."

"This feller ya drug outta the mud; do ya think he might of belonged to the horse with all the theater things on it?"

"I couldn't tell you for sure Tucker; I've never thought on it that way. He's such a tenderfoot; I'd never peg him for a dry gulcher."

"How tall is he? Is he about as tall as the shooter that shot Cord? Think back now and picture him in the brush where the shooter was running. What did you see?"

"I saw a wedged faced feller with a big nose and the look on his face was like the one ol yeller had a-eating that mouse out by the well that day. I reckon he's shorter than Luther and the rest of the descriptions of Half-a-Bob don't match Luther at all. Besides Luther is traveling with a wagon train making eyes at a little girl in a blue dress."

"Alright we'll skip over Luther right now; we'll wait and see if he shows up here. I don't want you killing the dry-gulcher; we also want the ones who paid him to shoot Pa."

Matt continued. "I'm thinking that he's already here and is being hid by his friends; suppose I ride out of town like I'm out searching the range for signs of him. He might see that as a good time to get me; my guess is he's been paid to shoot all of us. If I'm right he'll make a try for me and you can get a rope on him while he's stalking me."

"I don't know Matt; what if I don't see him and he gets in behind you?"

"We need to flush him out some way, anyway he could hide out and shoot me in the back right here in town."

The Ten Dollar Road

"I reckon that's so; it's a sure nuff good possibility, we'll have to set this up right. I'll need to be where I can cover you all the time."

"If you ride out ahead of me, you could wait till I come by and drop in behind, but stay off the trail to one side and keep out of sight. Whoever falls in behind me, you could get behind and keep me covered."

Tucker asked, "How far we gonna go? If he don't stumble on to the fact that you're leaving we could ride for nothing for a long ways."

"We'll ride east for two days; if we don't have him by then we'll come on back."

"Let's go hang around a couple of joints; have a couple drinks and spread the word that you're a-fixing to ride out tomorrow." Tucker grinned, "We might even find a friendly poker game to pass the time."

Matt and King left before sunrise and Matt let the big gray horse amble along at a pace of his choosing. Where the big grey horse went, the pack horses followed. He knew Tucker was already out there watching and he wanted Hatchet Face to have time to get his possibles and his soogan together and follow him. He knew one thing, one of these days he was going to walk Hatchet Face and those that hired him under some ropes.

Mouse pranced a little and pulled at the bit, it was easy to see he was eager to travel. When they stepped out towards the trail, the big gray horse liked it. King was running ahead casting back and forth from one side of the street to the other; judging from how fast his tail wagged he was having a grand ole time. At the edge of town, there was a small hovel where the Vargas family lived with six kids and a small Mexican hairless dog. When the tiny mutt saw King, he spread his front legs in an aggressive manner and his shrill bark announced that he ruled in this end of town. When Matt had ridden closer with King by his side, the little rascal was still challenging King. Matt laughed and called to him "ya got more guts than you have sense." The hairless midget rushed at King and King just acted like he weren't there and eyes straight ahead of him trotted on by.

Matt chuckled and said "Good boy, King." However, King never looked back and Matt knew to get quiet.

Tucker wasn't out there in front of Matt; he was lying up close to the sidewalk of the gunsmith's shop. He was lucky to be alive. He'd stumbled whilst walking past the shop; his toe had caught a nail that'd almost worked its way out of the boardwalk. He flung his arm out and shoved his hand again the wall but had almost gone down to his knees. A gun bellowed from the tall brush and scrub oaks that grew on a small ground swell that was across the street and back of the eating house. He instantly recognized the sound of a sharps 56 caliber sharpshooter's rifle. All one of those things needed to be a cannon was to be on wheels. The back shooter had used that same weapon on Pa. That feller had out foxed them; he had figured it out that Matt's leaving was a trap and had pert near collected his scalp. Tucker squirreled around on his hands and knees to the side of the building, but now he was between a rock and a hard place; if'n he moved that feller might still be there and shoot him. If'n he stayed that bushwhacker might ease around and slip up behind him. As it was, he was in a dark place beside the wall of the building and didn't know what to do.

Folks who had heard the shots were sticking their heads out to see what was happening, the sheriff come running carrying his six- gun in his hand. Tucker managed to get to his feet even though his knees felt wobbly and blood was running down his leg. He leaned against the building for support. He heard a horse leave out a-running and knew the shooter was gone.

"You there," the sheriff shouted. "Ya get your hands in the air."

Tucker figured if he let go the building he would fall; he compromised, he lifted one hand and hung on with the other' n.

"I need to hold on sheriff," he explained. "I think I took one in the leg."

The sheriff had been ready to fix a cell for Tucker but calmed down a mite when he explained about looking for Hatchet Face.

"I want you and that quick shoot 'n brother of yours outta here and I mean today."

Tucker stayed calm, "Sheriff Harr, that feller ambushed my Pa and killed him and we are not leaving till we've collected him and the ones that hired him. Now we have thirty-seven hands working for us. Every one of them ex-soldiers with plenty of bark on 'em; if you make a big hurrah outta this you'll have to deal with more guns than quills on a porcupine. We've told you about Half a Bob or Hatchet Face as my brother calls him; ya know him and you're not going to pick him up. So we'll stay till we find him!"

"Teal, I'm not scared of anybody; you included, but I ain't seen no proof yet that he's done anything."

"You're a double dyed liar! My brother saw him and if you're trying to say he's lying, I'll put some lead in you right here and right now!"

"You can't call me a liar and live." Sheriff Harr backed up undoing the strap over the hammer of his colt.

"You are lying sheriff" a voice come out of the gathered crowd, "Your covering up for that lunatic brother of yours; you know he's a murdering back shooter and as cracked as an old pot."

There was a murmuring of agreement from the crowd.

"We'll tell you something else too; he's not staying here, we'll hang him ourselves."

"He's not guilty of anything; just because he's different doesn't make him a killer."

"Oh, he's a killer all right. He's a murdering back shooting, sidewinder. Ever since he's come back from the war he has been as crazy as a bed bug. Everyone knows how much he gets for a killing. We used to think he was just being loco till he showed everyone the wad that he carried. If he comes back to this town we're gonna hang him ourselves!"

"My brother won't be coming back here; I'll see too that. You folks seem to forget he's a decorated war hero and was wounded twice in the war."

"Yeh, he was shot in the head one time too many."

The lawman turned on his heels and deliberately shouldered his way through the crowd. Everyone knew he was shamed, angry and hunting a reason to take it out on somebody, so they opened a path for him and watched him leave, head down, shoulders slumped and defeated.

"If'n he comes back here we'll stretch his neck for him." hollered a cowhand; and there was yells of agreement.

What was worrying Tucker was that Matt was out there expecting him to be watching his back and he weren't there? He kept urging the doc. "Could ya hurry this up? My kid brother is expecting me to be guarding his backside and won't know I ain't there."

"You're not running off anywhere," cautioned the Doctor. "If you plan on keeping that leg you will need medication and rest. Gangrene is easily acquired and hard to get rid of. Most of the time you just loose the limb."

Tucker knew it was good advice but Matt was counting on him; what if Matt was killed because he depended on me Tucker worried. He determined to go anyway but when he tried to stand up, the pain was so unbearable that he was not able to stand it.

"I believe your brother will do fine, you should have more faith in his abilities. He appears to be young but his actions are beyond his years. In fact he has shown a degree of maturity that is amazing for one so young." When Tucker thought of the hours and hours each day Matt had spent in practice, he was reassured in his mind and felt better about not being able to be there with him.

CHAPTER THIRTEEN

Matt was lollygagging along and checking for the possible places where he could be ambushed. He did as he'd been taught; he focused with his eyes but he focused with his mind as well. He projected a picture of the shooter through his eyes and concentrated on looking for a match. Like a man hunt 'n deer, he keeps the form of the deer in his mind and focuses on a match. A man that doesn't do that doesn't see the deer. He will not see the ears in the brush nor the standing deer in the tree line. Because he's not staying focused on what a deer looks like, he can't see the deer.

The afternoon passed quickly and Matt paused for some coffee, bacon and pan biscuits. He had a feeling of being watched but passed it off as nerves. He hadn't seen the reflection of the glass that was focused on him, he didn't know about the eyes following his every move. Twice there had been rifle sights fixed on him but the distance was close to a mile and the shooter didn't want to make a wayward shot and give himself away to a knowing Matt Teal; he would wait. Matt was looking for the reason for the raised hairs on his neck. There was somebody out there; he could feel him. Every physical sense was wide awake and searching; twice he looked at everything in reach of his eyes. Hurriedly he put his gear together, doused his fire and placed his possible bag behind Mouse's saddle. Keeping as low to the ground as possible he used Mouse as a shield and led the big gray horse back to the trail. The watchful eye of the shooter was following him and he wondered a-loud "I wonder how he tagged me; he sure didn't see me."

He waited till his intended victim was out of sight and then keeping to the low ground he moved to find a better spot for a good shot.

King would run by Mouse's side awhile and then go back to casting back and forth through the brush. Matt just let him run, whilst he figured on how to out fox whoever was following him. It could be Tucker but somehow he didn't figure on it. If'n it'd been Hatchet Face wouldn't he have made a try for him? Every nerve in him was keyed up tight and his eyes were doggedly searching for anything that was out of kilter.

He pulled up and dismounted, because he needed to do something different. If'n he rode on he was asking for trouble and besides that he needed to know where Tucker was; he decided he would hide and wait awhile. He walked Mouse behind a house sized boulder that hid him and where there was enough grass for the horses to graze on and still be out of sight.

He built a small fire up again the rock where the light wouldn't show and put a kettle of water on with some jerky in it. He climbed to the top of the boulder and lay flat while he checked everything, every tree, every bush, every cactus, every ground swell or dip; looking for a hand, an arm or foot showing, watching for movement, he couldn't make out anything outta kilter but still he knew from deep inside that something weren't right. His nerves were as tight as a bow string and he became more and more aware that he could die out here; that the danger was very real. Just one mistake would end it; there would be no second chances. He set on a log and remembered what his pa had said, "When ya are puzzled set still; nine times out of ten the answer will come to you." Matt finished eating and knew he had to go a different direction.

His searching eyes found a small drainage depression close by him, that was sheltered by the rock and tall grasses. It looked to be just deep enough to hide him and it headed towards a deeper rift. From a distance it would look level and flat and he would not be seen. Mouse and the pack horses were grazing contently and they would stay put unless disturbed and King was standing guard by Mouse. Matt took his canteen and a few necessities then switched to his moccasins and started crawling down the crevice searching for a better position to spot his enemy.

He crawled for the better part of an hour and the small ditch led to a narrow trench where he could walk if he stayed bent over with his head below the top. It was doubtful if the drainage gully he was in could be seen any better than the small ditch he'd been in. The gully soon turned into a gorge that was less than a quarter of a mile in length and a few hundred feet in width at its widest point; it most likely looked level from a distance. There was a small river running through it and his thought was that this would be a perfect place to protect Mouse. He retraced his path until he could see Mouse in the distance and whistled. In minutes King came slipping along in front of Mouse his big frame at a half crouch; the ruff around his neck was standing out stiff and it was plain he felt the tension and danger.

In minutes Matt had them in a natural corral; there was a river on one side, a dead end gorge on the other where he piled some brush at the entrance. And then he slipped into the bordering trees without a branch being disturbed or a twig snapping.

He glided through the trees, moving slow, climbing a tall tree now and then trying to spot his enemy. Then he got a whiff of wood burning but he did not see any smoke. There was only a whisper of sound that was much like a cough and a cautioning shush. Silently he slipped to where he could see the camp. Even looking straight at it the average cowhand would have missed it. Right smack dab in the middle of a thicket; the only way in was on your belly and crawling through heavy root growth.

There were a half dozen warriors squatting around a hand sized fire whose smoke was being dissipated and scattered by overhead branches. One of those warriors was the Kickapoo Matt had found injured on the trail. This was a war party and not a hunting party. They were painted for battle and there were no women or children.

With a killer hunting him and a bunch of mad injuns who would likely kill anybody they could reach he figured to hide for a while. Backing away whilst looking for a hidey hole he started to worry about Mouse being found when he purt near stepped on King. The big dog's eyes were fixed on the spot where the Injuns were but there weren't no sound coming outta his mouth and Matt didn't have to worry about him making any noise, but he was poised for attack. Matt took a step back and laid his hand on the big dog's head, together they started creeping back towards where they'd left Mouse.

King crept away following rabbit tracks; not now, Matt wanted to tell him but he didn't dare make a sound, with a grim feeling that fate was about to turn bad he followed King, not wanting to be separated now even though it meant crawling on his belly.

They dead ended against a pile of rocks that was almost hill sized and there was a overhanging cliff hidden by scrub oaks; smaller trees, and brush surrounded by tall grasses. They had located a place to hide above and overlooking the basin where they'd left Mouse.

"Ya move purty good for a younker." A whisper broke through Matt's silent scrutiny.

Matt whirled; drew, and was on one knee on the ground in an eye blink.

"Whew, you are fast," said the whisper. And then Matt saw him; a wizened little old man squatted in the tall grass. "I been watching ya; figured ya for a goner when ya got close to the bucks on the war path." He was holding on to a buffalo gun and it were pointed at Matt. "Figured I'd have me a nice looking grey horse outta the deal, most likely I'd of had to shoot that monster ya call a dog first."

Matt's forty four was still pointed at the old man and his heart was still pounding. The hammer was back and only needed a nudge to fire.

"My names Henry," The old feller said laying the rifle down "And I'm sure glad ya didn't shoot me. I didn't figure on ya being so blame fast."

"My names Matt Teal I'm from over at Two Tracks. Ya purt near lost your head just now and if them Injuns spot us ya might lose it anyway. We'd have a real fight on our hands; them's' Kickapoo's."

"I reckoned to sit tight till they light out; are them your pack horses moving in down there?"

Matt looked down at Mouse and sure enough the pack animals were headed towards Mouse. The packs though were still back up there behind the rocks where he'd first got off the trail. "Reckon so, they like to stay close to my horse."

"They got no packs. That means ya got no food, no coffee or nothing."

"I got packs close by, as soon as those Indians move out."

"Well that's good 'cause I ain't one to share."

"Friendly cuss ain't ya."

"I start out giving ya a cup of coffee and then I feed ya and then we get friendly and then I don't know how to get rid of ya. It's easier just to not start it."

Matt laughed and took out his sling, there were some big fat squirrels running everywhere; in a couple of eye blinks there was four of'm ready for the skinning and not a noise was made.

"I brought 'em down you fix 'em and make some biscuits as soon as them Injuns leave."

"Well I'll swan if'n ye might not be worth sump 'em after all boy. Can ya bring down a man with that?"

"David did!"

He stared at Matt for a bit and then he chuckled, "Have ya killed a lion and a bear?"

"As a matter of fact I have; but not with a sling. But a sling will develop the speed and power of a 30-30 slug after two swings, and with a steel ball I wouldn't be afraid to tackle a bear. Pa said that in olden times in Europe, armies had whole companies whose weapon was slings and that they was more feared than the archers because of the speed they could sling with."

"How about that big Iron on your hip, are ya any good with that?"

"I can use it if'n I have too."

"I'll just bet ya can boy. Watch close now them Injuns are moving out and if'n any of them come this way ya use that sling, we don't want no noise made to drag the rest of'm in here on us."

Matt watched them creep out of their camp and slither through the tall grasses but they all went the other direction. And after a bit they were mounted and jogging right out like they didn't have a care in the world. He thought what he could do with his Winchester but the old man sensed what he was thinking and held his hand out in a stopping motion. "Let 'em go boy, we got no dealings with such as them."

"I hope we don't," Matt said fervently, "them are fight 'n fools and there ain't no quit in them."

At least they didn't have to talk in whispers anymore and that made it easier to exchange information.

Roasted squirrel and the gravy that was made from the drippings and biscuits went real good, he figured if'n that old geezer could cook like that that he was worth knowing. He let his eyes meet the old man's watering pale blue eyes.

"Henry, how come you're out here instead of being in town?"

"I've spent almost all of my life out in these woods and I don't feel at home in town. Truth is I could live with my son and his wife but she don't want me; I'm not civilized enough to move as I'm told to move like my boy does, and she rules the roost. I chew tobacco and don't take enough baths and I don't load her down with silver from the mine I told her I had."

"She actually believes ya have a silver mine?"

"I do have; it don't produce much and ya really have to work for it, but it's enough to keep me alive." Then switching matters around he asked "Watch 'ya doing here your own self?"

So Matt told him the whole thing and even gave a purty good word picture of what the shooter looked like.

"Pears to me that ya need to set a spell; that back shooter is most likely on your trail right now and from what you've said I'd figure he's good at back shooting. Let him come to you only let the trap be one that ya set your own self."

"Yes sir, I can see the need of that but finding the right place to set the trap is what I'm doubtful about."

"Ya need to be hid and to have a good clear line of sight all around you. There's a limestone cave back away from the river a couple of miles down the river. It's among a lot of rocks and brush and the whole place is covered with scrub trees. I think I'm the only one that knows it's there; even the injuns don't ever use it. Best part is it's big inside and there's a water fall in there that feeds a good sized pond and a runoff that goes on underground. Ya can hide your horses in there. We can set up a good watch from in there."

"How big a river is this? Is the cave right on the river?"

"It's a fair sized river; this is the Guadalupe, it ends up in the gulf and that's a far piece. The cave is purt near a half mile back from the rivers bank. This is hill country and there's a lot of hiding places in these hills. That's what makes it so dangerous for you to search for him and why ya need to let him come to you."

CHAPTER FOURTEEN

The cave turned out to be everything that was said about it and more.

"How come it's so light in there?" Matt asked.

"At the other end there's places where the wall is so thin it has slits clear through to the outside; like skinny windows."

"Then how come no one can see that this is a cave?"

"At that end ya look a couple of hundred feet straight down a shear bluff, so straight, there ain't no way to climb it. When ya look at it from the valley on that side it looks like the side of a big rock plateau that has come to a point on top."

"What's over there?" asked Matt.

"Small valley, mostly farm land and there's a little town called Huntley. Mostly nice folks live there. A big general store sells about everything. There's a couple of saloon's there, the kind of places where farmers gather and talk crops. They've got a town marshal name of Big John, feller in his early thirties; he has a name for being tough and I figure he's not someone to take lightly. They got a bank, but I doubt there's much money in it. They do have good food there; I've gnawed my way through a steak there a time or two and the fixings are plumb satisfying. "Why don't we sashay on down

117

there?" Matt asked. "I'm tired of camp cooking and maybe we might come on something about that Hatchet Faced feller I'm looking for."

"I reckon I could force another good steak down if'n it's for a good reason." laughed Henry.

Huntley was not a busy town. There was a wagon being loaded at the Mercantile, a few horses were tied to the hitching rail in front of the "Salty Dog" saloon and eating-place. There was a pinto tied to the hitching rail in front of the gunsmith's shop. Matt's eyes swept over the main part of Huntley as they rode in. There was three riders coming in from the south and Matt had already sorted them out. They had the look of riding the back trails; their holsters were tied down, their dusters were buttoned back to give room to reach their six guns, their eyes were busy tallying up and sorting out the town. It was their horses that were a complete give-away; cowhands didn't ride horses that cost as much money as their mounts must of.

Matt reined Mouse to the rail in front of the Salty Dog, it had been a sudden move and Henry looked startled. "We lose something here?"

"Get down easy like, I know one of them fellers and he's a dyed in the wool bad man, be easy and don't attract any attention." Henry stood beside Matt at the hitch rail. "Is there something wrong boy, are you backing away from them hard cases?"

"Yeah, I shot the tall one in the back down by Two Track."

Henry stepped back and grunted an ugly snarl. "Ya better have a real good reason for this young's, I don't cotton to back shooters." "His name's Johnny Tieg and he robbed a bank."

Matt told the whole story and waited for Henrys thoughts on it.

"Well I reckon you done right although I pretty much figure it like your Pa, it weren't good judgment. Now you're faced with a hombre who'll shoot ya on sight." Matt answered. "I don't reckon I'll wait for that to happen, I'll just amble on down there and make him face me now."

"Well now, wait a minute let's think this over; suppose we let the town marshal know who he is and how he feels about you. It could be there's a reward out for him and Big John might like to collect it. Anyway, it never hurts to have the town on your side when there's a shootout."

Matt thought about and agreed with it. "Big John's office is on the other side of them; how we gonna get past them to tell the marshal?"

"You stay here and I'll go, they don't know me and I won't have no trouble getting past them."

Johnny and his partners had already walked into the mercantile and Henry walked by gazing through the windows just as if he didn't have a care in the world. King had installed his self across the threshold of the entrance to the Salty Dog. Matt was leaning up against the hitching rail watching towards where Henry had gone. It weren't long till Henry was back.

"Big John said as far as he was concerned them fellers had just as much right to be here as we have and he didn't have no reward poster on him. If'n there was any trouble he'd throw us in jail, in fact he figured we'd over-stayed our welcome and had best leave now."

"I don't figure the man acting that way, was he drinking?" Matt questioned.

"Not so much as I could tell it if'n he was."

They were mounting their horses when shots could be heard down at the mercantile store; "come on" Henry shouted and rushed into the Salty Dog with Matt plumb on his heels. They stopped at the window and watched Johnny and his partners rush by. They was using their quirts hard and fast trying to get the most outta their mounts. Matt looked at Henry and nodded his head at a table where they sat down. "We'd best sit down for a bit till that law man chases after Johnny; the first thing that will cross his mind will be to throw us in the clink."

"He sure won't want anybody to know he could've been there and wasn't." added Henry.

Matt said, "as long as we gotta be here I'm ordering me the biggest steak they got."

"Make that two and get us a gallon of coffee," chuckled Henry.

There was more hullabaloo out front as the marshal and six or so town's people went racing by.

"Well that's about all the men in town," Henry observed. "We can eat up now."

"I think we should be gone a-for he gets back. If he hasn't caught them, I don't want to be here. He just might figure we'd do just fine for fill in's". Henry laughed, "I've heard he can be a mighty hard man Matt, for us not to be here when he gets back is probably the smartest thing we can do."

The front door opened with a bang and when Matt looked up there stood Hatchet Face with a gun in his hand, instinctively Matt did the move he had practiced since he was a young 'n; he dropped and rolled pulling his gun as he rolled. Hatchet Face fired and missed, Matt fired and hit him in the upper arm. He was slammed back again the doorpost, shocked by the way things had gone. Holding the hurt arm with his other hand, he dropped his gun and ran, he had expected to kill Matt and things had gone wrong, he was hit and didn't know how bad. By the time Matt made it to the door Hatchet Face had flung himself in his saddle and was running like a scalded dog. He hadn't paid attention to that big mutt lying across the door when he was ready to burst in on Matt, except for aiming a kick at him to make him move.

He hadn't seen the way King tensed up and the instant anger in his eyes.

But he sure paid attention when he come running out; that blamed big dog had almost jerked him out of the saddle and had pert near bit his right arm in two. The pain from the dog's teeth was worse right now than the pain from Matt's bullet. Blood ran freely from the slash in his right arm as well as the bullet wound in his left arm. That dog scared him; he wouldn't let up, and was still trying to bring down the horse. His horse was fighting to stay upright and still run. King almost had them down by pushing against the horse with all of his enormous strength and his one hundred fifty plus pounds of weight. However, the horse knew his business and turned suddenly, and kicked King so hard it knocked him across the road.

There was blood on the doorpost and some on the floor; it looked like Hatchet Face was hit pretty bad, but it hadn't slowed him down none when it came down to leaving outta there. What was meaningful to Matt was that he had seen the horse Hatchet Face was riding and it wasn't the one Luther had been using. Just to be sure, Matt examined the tracks and the tracks were different. Henry stopped Matt to keep him from following after him.

"Hold on there young feller, this is a setup. There'll be an ambusher a wait 'n for you just a hop, skip, and a jump, down the road there somewhere. Ya got him now and he's coming to you, we'll set our own trap now." Matt struggled for a little bit, his face was flushed and he had eagerness written all over him but he settled down and listened to Henry and knew he was making sense.

By the time, Matt's attacker had got out of town he was woozy and needed help bad, but he wasn't down and out yet. His sidekick had a brother who was a sheriff and he would help them. All he needed was a place to hide and time to heal. Half a Bob Harr was out there waiting for him, and when he didn't show up as planned, Half a Bob would come looking for him. He knew he could depend on him. They'd been sharp shooters under the same commander; they'd fought together and sometimes bled together, always watching out for each other. He knew Half a Bob Harr would never let him down. But everything had turned dark now, with millions of tiny dots in his eyes. He fell sideways from the saddle, his head cleared for a bit until the pain hit again, he wished Half a Bob would hurry and come.

King was lying off the road in the brush, his side was caved in and he was bleeding from the broken ribs. His instinct was in-born and he had pushed his way as far into the thick brush as he could. He felt the blood running inside and the pain was making him whimper. Every instinct was telling him he was dying and to hide and die privately. He left a trail of blood and pressed down weeds, but he wasn't aware of that and the blood loss let his consciousness drift away.

Matt and Henry left; hurried by the desire to be gone before the sheriff returned. They were reading the tracks that Hatchet Face and King had left. They came across where the dog was hiding before they ever got to where Hatchet Face was laying on the ground. Not knowing how close they came to ending the chase. Matt waded through the weeds until he found King; the big dog's every breath was a struggle and life was almost gone. Desperately he began pulling the weeds from around him to clear a place to work. "Henry, would you bring that black case from behind my saddle?"

"Alright, but are you sure? It might be easier on the dog to just shoot him without doing a lot of handling. Every time you touch him, it hurts him and he ain't gonna make it anyway."

"I aim to give him every chance I can to help him to live, hand me that bottle of laudanum would you?" He poured painkiller down him and felt the tenseness relax while he cut away the bloody hair from his side; two ribs were broken with the broken ends pressing in towards his lungs.

First thing he needed to do, Matt figured, was to get the bleeding stopped; to do that he needed to relieve the pressure from the broken ribs.

"I got to get them ribs lined up." He appealed to Henry.

Henry motioned for Matt to move over and selected one of the knives from the case; he rolled his sleeve up and splashed some whisky over the wound. Matt's part was to keep the pain killer going down when it was needed while Henry removed the part of the ribs that was crushed. Using the big needle and catgut, he closed off the bleeding and sewed the wound up tight. Matt was awed by the skill Henry showed. "Henry that was as good as any doctor could've done; I really owe you, I appreciate it and if there's anything I can ever do for you just let me know because I reckon I'd do purt near anything for you."

"I don't think we done your dog any favors, he's missing about half of a couple of ribs and it leaves a soft place where he needs protection. It's gonna take time to heal. Now then, I don't want to hang around here while he gets well. If'n he does get well; ya can catch up with me in German Town."

CHAPTER FIFTEEN

Matt wished he wouldn't go but Henry was set in his ways and the truth was he didn't know Matt that well and there weren't any reason for him to stay. King had a tight body wrap fastened all the way around him and was getting lots of salt water poured down him. Salt water was one of Rosa's remedies for loss of blood and over the next week Matt got as much of it down him as possible. It seemed as though he wasn't gonna make it but Matt wouldn't quit, he set there for two weeks before King was up and moving some. It had taken a lot of meat broth, special feeding, and a lot of encouraging petting before King would even try.

They started traveling slow and cautious and every little bit they'd stop so King could rest; but they did better every day and the time did come when King was able to travel most of every day. Hatchet Face hadn't had it as good; he was there, where he fell, all that day and the next one. When Half a Bob finally found him, his arms were purple and black and swelled up almost twice normal size. "What had happened to Joseph?" He had never thought of him as Hatchet Face; although he knew other folks called him that. He had warned him to leave that Teal family alone, now look at the mess he was in! Where

125

to take him was the question? He wouldn't live through a long trip; Huntley had a doctor but it would be a good guess that Joseph had been in trouble there, and he couldn't take him to German Town. His brother had already told him not to come back there or to let Joseph come back there. He knew from looking at the mangled arm that gangrene had already set in on the left side. The infection had covered the arm and there was purple running across the shoulder.

Half a Bob knew the left arm had to come off if his partner was going to live; and the right arm was looking bad. But what would his amigo want? Death might be preferable to losing his arm, or arms. How would he get the arm off? He didn't have anything to cut or saw with. Finally he rode to Huntley and brought the doctor back with a story of a shoot-out with outlaws. The doctor didn't believe him but was wise enough not to reveal his doubts. The doctor was doubtful that Joseph would even live. He was almost dead when he first saw him, and cutting off the arm would most likely kill him. But there was no time to delay; if he didn't take it off now the inflammation would kill him anyway. He sighed and reached for his bag. "These blame fools make calamities out of their bodies and then pray for help."

The arm came off with no problems but his life signs were so low even the smallest move would kill him so Half a Bob built him a shelter of young limbs with ferns for sides and a roof. Later he brought supplies and more bandages. He'd been worried the doctor would tell the town marshal but he didn't. Half a Bob had paid the good doctor a couple of gold eagles and that bought them some time.

Matt, King, Mouse, and the pack horses all headed back to German Town. Matt knew he'd put a bullet in Hatchet Face's arm but he didn't know how bad he was hurt. He felt like he better go and find Tucker and he'd just have to chance it that there might be an ambush up ahead. He rode right by where Half a Bob had Joseph hid out. Both of those men were asleep, one was worn out and the other 'n was purt near dead. Matt's mind was on King and where he might find Tucker and he rode right by the tracks that would have led him to his enemy.

They spent the first night in the cave that Henry and he had stayed in. After that they stayed in close to the river till they come across the boulder that he'd hid behind. German Town weren't that far now and it was mostly flat land between the boulder he was hid behind and the town where he was going. If there was an ambush planned it'd be around here. He dismounted and switched his boots for his moccasins; keeping hold of the reins he walked by Mouse's shoulder, a pack horses covered his left side, and sheltered like he was he had time to see any possible spot a shooter might like to use. It was a long walk into town, but he got there safe. "Better slow than not at all," he told himself.

He hadn't known about Tucker till he saw him with his leg all bandaged up. Tuckers face lit up, "Where ya been, I've been worrying about ya being gone so long."

"I don't even know where to start; I did come face to face with the bushwhacker, he purt near sent my saddle home, it was that close," Matt grimaced.

"I'm shore glad ya come through alright little brother; y'all find that where there's gunplay there's gonna be some close ones. Did ya collect his scalp?"

"No, but I got lead in him and he was hurt bad, I reckon he was needful of a saw-bones."

"Was ya close to where he could find help?"

"We was in a little town called Huntley; close to the Pedernales River, small town, about the size of Two Track. But he took out of there like his tail was on fire and I don't think he would go back there."

"That would depend on how bad he was hurt wouldn't it? If he were hurt real bad and if he had a companion helping him he might just hole up and have his partner bring a sawbones to him. Did ya watch the trail to see if he set in somewhere?"

"No." admitted Matt, "I reckon I'd better go back for another look."

Tucker's voice was grim. "We'll both go this time; my leg is good enough I can ride."

Matt suddenly realized he'd not showed any interest in Tuckers leg bandage. "I must have been so set on what I was doing I never paid no mind to what happened to you."

"Some-one laid up for me in the bushes over behind the eat 'n house and got some lead into my leg. I'm just now getting over it enough to walk a little."

Matt looked at Tuckers leg and figured that he using it before it was healed would be the wrong thing to do. "Tucker, you've got a real bad leg and King has some broken ribs, how about you staying put and keeping King with you? I can back track lots faster by myself." Tucker knew he was supposed to stay as still as possible and Matt was talking sense.

"That's the biggest dog I have ever seen in all my life and when he pulls his lips back into that chicken eat 'n grin like he's doing now; I don't know whether he's being friendly or about to eat me."

Matt laughed "He just likes you, if'n he makes supper outta you, I'll whip him real hard."

Tucker didn't laugh. "I'm dog-gone serious, I'm not sure about him. But I'll keep my gun handy and we'll give it a try. Come on let's go eat and then ya get some sleep, tomorrow morning is soon enough to start hunt 'n again."

Matt had a hard time making King stay with Tucker; twice he followed after Mouse, even begging with his eyes trying to soften Matt's determination to make him stay. But he just weren't ready to travel yet and Matt wouldn't give in to him. Finally he stood in the middle of the trail and whined piteously whilst Matt rode away. Tucker laughed at him, "he's trying to work on your sympathies, don't let him trick ya."

But Matt was feeling like he was letting his best friend down even when he knew it was the right thing to do. As he rode off King howled like his heart was breaking and Matt had to grit his teeth and keep riding.

He was going to start at Huntley even though he didn't figure he would find any trace of Hatchet Face there. But he knew he'd got lead in him, he'd seen blood on the door where he'd fell against it whilst he was getting away. So it was possible he'd circled back and seen the doctor there in Huntley. The question was should he go around and follow the river or go straight across country. Which way was he going to leave himself open to ambush and which way was he most likely to find his man? Just how bad off was his quarry and where was he?

Joseph was moaning, twisting and writhing in pain but the doctor was afraid to give him more pain killer. He threshed back and forth on his bed of grass; they were still hid out in the brush and it looked like they would be for a few days. Half a Bob was inclined to leave him; because the noise he was making would surly give their hiding place away, and that Teal kid didn't look to be the forgiving kind. Trouble was ya just didn't throw down on someone you'd fought beside, shared danger with, shared your food with; also the time when ya needed a doc in a hurry he had carried ya in on his shoulder to the medical tent; unmindful to the zing of the bullets flying all around them. How could ya close your eyes to him now? Half a Bob sighed and knew whatever fate had in store for them; they were in it together. It was needful to start a fire, they had to eat and he needed coffee real bad; building a fire couldn't make things any worse, anybody in a quarter mile around them could hear the cries of pain that Joseph couldn't keep himself from expressing. The doc had put a limit on how much laudanum he could give him because if he gave him too much over a long time it could kill him. He just wished Joseph would wake up, if'n he was awake he might be able to control those screeches of pain.

Matt figured he would cut across country and save time getting to Huntley, he was sure Hatchet Face wasn't there but he needed a place to start and at the same time he didn't want to leave any stone unturned. So he rode Mouse across the small hill country watching for Indians as well as the man he was looking for. He passed through miles of tall dry grass that would have been knee high had he dismounted.

"There could be a whole tribe of them critters in this grass and I'd never see them," he muttered. The very thought of which made him twice as watchful! He was wishful of King right now; King would smell them injuns a mile away if'n there was any. That night he camped right out in the middle of all that grass, he dug a good deep fire pit and found some rocks to line it with. He gathered up buffalo chips and started a fire; the pit was deep enough that if he had a small enough fire no-body would be able to spot it and there wasn't any fire danger. Having ate a good meal of pan biscuits and red gravy, he set there using his saddle as a chair and sipped his coffee; if'n he weren't man hunting he could sure enjoy this time of being alone in the peace and quiet of the night noises. A coyote yipping and a prairie hen calling to her chicks with the light flashing from the fireflies made him smile sleepily thinking about rolling up in his blanket. There was a twig snapped to his right and he rolled into a prone position with a gun in his hand. Set 'n right across the fire from him was that Kickapoo he'd patched up a while back. "Pale face boy not live long out here." The injun smiled. "White man hiding in grass, a rifle shot away. He follows you all day and is going to take your scalp tonight. He is good at taking scalps; he is wearing Kickapoo scalps on his belt."

Matt jumped to his feet. "I'll go take care of him right now."

The Kickapoo warrior chief pointed towards the ground "Ínenia Clipatapino! In my language that means squat right there. My warriors will have him and that means death for him."

Matt squatted down and asked, "How come you speak our language so well?" "I was born in the north; a place called Wisconsin and lived there for many years. There was a teacher that lived among us and my father, who was chief, made all of us go to his school. Then, being wanderers, we moved south but there were the Apaches and we moved again and again until we ended up here. Then I kill chief and I became war chief. What does pale faced boy seek?"

So Matt told him of his search for Bruisers killer, and told him about the search from the beginning to the present. When he told of the part of being buried alive the Injun laughed so hard he rocked back and forth with glee.

Matt burned with resentment; it hadn't been funny to him. "I wasn't laughing, it weren't funny being buried alive; the dirt was so heavy I couldn't breathe, I couldn't even wiggle my toes."

"Much funny me," the chief sputtered. "Later, it be funny you. Great Spirit not finished with you yet; so you live because He says so."

Matt thought about that and nodded his head in agreement, "I asked Him to let me live; I didn't know if He even heard me or not. Do you think I live because God answered my prayer?"

"I believe He help you."

Matt wanted to talk some more about it but a sound of running horses brought him to his feet. Six braves circled the camp, riding round and round the fire, dragging a body at the end of a rope. One of the braves was holding a man's head high and yelling a victory chant. Matt felt his stomach turn sour and quiver as he recognized old cast eye, the one he'd had trouble with at the saloon. Seeing that he was being watched the brave jumped up and stood on his pony's back still holding the separated head.

"You must close your fists and raise your arms shaking them in victory," The chief told him, "do not insult brave by not showing him what a great warrior you think he is."

The yelling died down and the brave still carrying the head stopped in front of the chief. He said something to the chief and backed his horse away.

"He says, man not fun, he not last."

Then the Chief explained, "This man killed our people to sell our scalps at the army post. He was told hunt Apaches, but he killed Mexicans, Kickapoo, and other Indians; army man not tells difference in scalps and Apache too dangerous to hunt."

"He was a bad 'n al 'right; he had a long drop and a short rope coming to him. I don't know if dragging him was any worse than hanging him; my people hang men like him." Matt replied.

"Him lucky it was Kickapoo who catch him; Apache would have hung him over fire head first till he goes crazy with pain. He screams all night before he die."

"I've heard about men dying like that, but I've never seen it. It would take a really mean critter to do a man that way."

"Apaches animals, they dance around man with his head to fire; they laugh and feel like big warriors. They treat Kickapoo same."

"Ya need better guns; if ya had some good carbines that carry a load of seventeen shots like mine ya wouldn't need to be afraid of the Apache." Matt's voice carried conviction.

"We know we need better guns. Will white boy bring us weapons?"

"I cannot buy a lot of weapons all at the same time; people would know what I was doing and punish me. But I can give you money to buy some from the gun runners in Mexico."

"We have gold and silver; we give you much gold to get us guns."

Matt looked at him as solemn as any judge, "I'd help ya except ya might have some braves that would use the rifles on white folks. I couldn't do that anymore than you would want to help me do something that could hurt the Kickapoo." The red man grabbed Matt's rifle. "Then I take this one!" Matt's six gun was instantly jammed in the injun's belly and the hammer was already back and ready to fire. He held out his hand and the chief reluctantly gave back the weapon.

"Now then, I give ya this rifle chief; ya can't take it from me but I give it to ya." The Chief took the Winchester and stared hard at Matt; then turning he turned his back to Matt leaving him to wish he were somewhere else. In showing that he wasn't weak enough to have something taken from him had he given offense? Had he hurt the red man's pride? He sure didn't need to make an enemy of him now; not surrounded by all these braves. Suddenly everything turned black and he slid to the ground, not seeing the injun with the wood club standing over him and grinning down at him. The chief grunted an order and Matt's guns and bed roll were taken from him. The next thing he knew was that he was lying on the hard ground and trussed up like a calf at a barbecue. Instant rage enveloped him and he looked to see where that Indian chief was, he was a Teal and nobody treated a Teal like this; not and live!

"White Boy wants talk with me?" Matt twisted his head around to find where he could see that sneaky deceiving red skin set 'n close by watching him.

"Why are you doing this? I saved your life and this is how you treat me? How can you even bring yourself to do this?"

"Because I am strong! A weak warrior would feel like he owed you but I am strong. I was strong when I killed my father and became chief!"

"Your father was the chief?"

"Yes, and I was strong enough to become chief."

"And your father, he knew you were going to kill him?"

"Yes, him become very angry at me. But I was strong and I killed him."

"Did you not have any feelings for him?"

"I have many feelings for my father; but I was strong enough to become chief."

Matt was silent for a moment; how could you reason with that kind of thinking?

Matt would try to be as strong.

"You'll get these ropes off me and do it now! If'n ya know what's good for you. I know you've seen the Teal ranch and so you must know my brothers will come after you with at least fifty well-armed experienced warriors. Unless ya want your whole tribe wiped out you'll cut me loose now. We even have a Gatling gun; they won't stop at the boarder like the Texas Police, they'll follow you till they've run you down."

"That is so," agreed the chief; "If they knew what happened to you, but they not know."

It suddenly come to Matt he best control his temper; threats would not help him now.

He fixed his eyes on the chief's eyes. "When I found you hurt and dying I took care of you. Is this the way you treat me when I treated you like a friend?"

"You helped me as my spirit much strong; your medicine weak. Your spirit not says no to my medicine."

"If my medicine so weak why do you need to tie me up?"

"White boy we are enemies, we not friends. I no take your hair because you not treat me as enemy."

"You know it is for me to find the killer who ambushed my pa."

"The one who you hunt for will be ours when sun comes up; he is also my enemy and he will die hard."

"So, am I going to die hard?"

"We sell you to brown robes in Mexico; they need strong young boys to work mine. I do not believe Great Spirit finished with you yet. I do not know how you will die."

"Well then I'm ahead of you; my brothers will kill you before the next full moon."

The Chief laughed, "Your brothers not find me."

Matt was left hogtied and hungry; there was a young calf being turned on a tree limb over the fire and whisky was flowing freely, but he didn't know where the whiskey came from unless they had took it from some wagon they'd captured. He was trying hard not to let his circumstances clog up his thinking. One angry word could get him killed, so when they made fun of him, or kicked him, and spit on him he just endured; trying to laugh when they laughed. The more they drank the louder they got so when the chief stumbled he asked him, "Why don't ya just send a messenger to the Apache's and invite them to come and kill you?"

He glared at Matt but he grabbed the whisky bottle and emptied it and ordered his braves to be quiet. And finally in their whisky stupor they slept. Matt couldn't sleep much; he kept waking up every hour or so. It felt like his ropes were too tight and his legs were numb.

CHAPTER SIXTEEN

Tucker and King were trying to track Matt. King had his nose in Mouse's tracks and Tucker was watching for any signs of hostiles. They came on where Matt had made a stop to build a fire and afterwards he had buried the ashes, "this was done yesterday." Tucker told King and King drew the corners of his mouth back in what looked like a smile; his eyes had a sparkle to them, King liked to be talked to. Then Tucker spotted injun tracks covering Matt's, "he's got company." His voice betraying his concern, "I make it to be at least six of them varmints sneaking around. I sure hope Matt's keeping a sharp lookout for them red devils. We best be picking them up and put 'em down if'n we are going to get there in time to help him." A couple of hours later they found the tracks ol' cast eye had made. It looked like he was staying with Matt's tracks, "well sir, King we got us a real puzzle here; who is this hombre that's put his-self in the middle of what we're doing."

When they found where cast eye had hid while he tried to get a good shot at Matt; Tucker was really troubled. He knew Matt was well trained and he hadn't heard a shot yet but still there was that nagging worry. Then he found where the Injuns had roped cast eye and drug him. He didn't know the hombre that they had put a rope on but he figured it was a sorry way for anybody to die. "King, we need to really be awake now; there's some bad red skins out there and they would like to get their ropes on another white man and I'll bet they would think that we would do just fine. Now you get out there and keep a good look out."

Kings eyes brightened and he watched Tuckers eyes expectantly; Tucker waved his hand and King bounded out front just as if he'd understood every word. Casting back and forth with his nose to the ground for any smell of Mouse and then he would stop, cock his head and listen intently, then he'd move forward, stop, and check again. Tucker had his glass out and was checking everything within his vision.

"Ya know King; I believe ya understand a lot more than you get credit for." They found where Matt had made his coffee and made some pan biscuits, there was even some scrap of biscuit laying there and King snatched it up and swallowed it all in one move.

"I wonder why Matt would have left sign like that laying around," pondered Tucker, "that ain't a bit like him." He slid outta his saddle and went inch by inch over all of the possible range he would have used as a campsite. He noticed a patch of grass that had the blades turned the wrong way and another that looked wadded up; he started pulling plugs of grass and a picture of what went on here developed. It was plain they had spent the night and that Matt had been tied up. He found where they buried the cook fire. They had hid things pretty well but not good enough. He was glad that Matt had dropped that bit of biscuit or he might not have stopped.

"Injuns got him King, they took him with them; about seven of'm I make it." He swung his arm out, "King, go find him!"

Again King took off at a trot and as the injuns didn't even try to hide their tracks, King was soon at a running lope. Tucker reined his horse in, dismounted and checked the tracks. He knew Mouse's tracks and he used them to go by. They were about three hours ahead of him but they wouldn't be for long.

They were headed south back towards Mexico or at least that direction, there could be almost anything that way; even outlaws sometimes had hideouts in one of the many limestone caves. A lot of stolen goods were sold or traded in the outlaw camps. There was a slave trade and the Injuns and outlaws often coming together to take advantage of the unwary and defenseless. Far to the south there were mines that used up men in a never-ending craving, strong and healthy men that soon become sick with the mine lung sickness and became dying invalids that are disposable and expendable. They were treated like the useless rock that surrounded the silver veins that threaded its way through the mines. The useless rock was crushed and hauled out of the way as was the used up men. The mine entrance was a Hugh maw with a never-ending appetite for more men and they didn't care where they came from or how they were obtained.

Matt knew nothing about the world outside the ranch life he was raised in; he knew little or nothing about slavery or mines. He wasn't worried about his tricky situation, because eventually one of them injuns was gonna make a mistake and it'd be goodbye injuns. Matt would be gone in an eye blink.

One thing for sure that Injun Chief had a reckoning coming to him and when he had the upper hand he was going to make sure he was one sorry injun. Matt didn't expect any outside help and didn't figure on Tucker even looking for him yet. One thing he might be able to do was that he still had his belt buckle gun. The buckle was leather covered and since it wasn't bright and shiny the Indians didn't take it from him. The other thing he had going for him was his boot knife; they hadn't even looked in his boots yet. They stopped and gathered around a campfire to have a pow wow or something, the Chief and some of the braves were at cross ways with each other, the Chief was angry, not liking the opposition and had set his head he was going to have his way. The braves were just as single-minded until the Chief used his knife on the most out spoken of the opposition; he was arguing with him and then quick as a wink, he stuck a knife in the hardheaded buck! There was complete silence except some of the other ones who'd been fussing with the Chief was moving back away from the ones that was facing the Chief. They'd plumb lost their eagerness to get their point across. Now, whatever the Chief said was right and proper.

"He sure knows how get the best of an argument," Matt thought. "I wonder what that was all about anyway." They threw the dead injun across the back of his horse and tied him on; they were gonna take him home and give him a proper send off. Matt thought that was strange; first he killed him and now he was gonna take him home and pay respect to him.

Matt didn't get to ride Mouse anymore, they tied a rope around Matt's neck and he begun a shuffling run too keep up with the injun who held the other end of the rope. Two hours later his legs started to cramp, by the time another hour went by his legs were in torment and his breaths were short and gasping. There was so much pain going through his body he was sure he was at deaths door. The sun was going down but he never noticed it, his chest felt like it was on fire and his breath came in great rasping sobs. There were heavy wobbly weights where his legs used to be. Everything went black and he fell; nobody acted as they cared and the rope had jerked tightly around his neck scraping it raw and shutting off his breath.

The Chief made them put him back on his horse. Repeating as loud as he could yell they wanted to sell him and they wouldn't be able to if he was damaged. That night when they made camp he was more dead than alive. He tried to tell them about the laudanum in his saddlebag but none of the braves would listen; so he asked to talk to the chief. However, there was a celebration with some whiskey from somewhere and dances to brag on their heroic acts and the Chief was as full of lies as the rest. Finally, when he needed to rest he came to talk.

"White boy want to talk with war chief? Are your brothers here to kill me yet?"

"If they was you'd know it because you'd be hiding in the brush."

"White boy lives because I say so; he dies when I say so. It's not wise to anger chief."

"It's not wise to anger Great Spirit, and you are treating me like a dog! I have medicine in my saddlebags, the same kind of medicine I helped you with. Would you get it for me please and untie my hands so I can doctor my wounds?"

"Because you helped me I will help you." And he untied Matt's hands, and while Matt was rubbing his hands to get some circulation going in his hands a brave brought him his saddle bags. While getting out the laudanum and salve he discovered his derringer was still in the inside pocket he had made for it. "I thank you Luther," he muttered to himself whilst hiding the little gun. He was flat out tempted to take a chance for freedom right then but his better judgment overcame the impulse and he set about repairing himself. At least he had something for the pain and some salve for the torn places in his hide. He had to make a move soon or he'd be dead anyway. He couldn't run like that another day.

He had almost finished doctoring himself when there was a great hullabaloo up by the campfire; he couldn't see from where he was at what was going on but they were sure happy about something. He took holt of a nearby braves arm. "What's going on?"

"We capture long time enemy!"

"Who? Apache?"

"No, a killer and a white scalp hunter, he's took his last Kickapoo scalp!"

"Who is he? Do you know his name? What does he look like?"

The brave took him by the arm and propelled him into the crowd that had gathered around to see the white enemy. And there stood Hatchet Face along with Half a Bob.

Matt saw the chief close by and instant rage drove away all reason; all conscience thought, and almost insane he hollered, "Chief let me kill him, it's my right!"

Joseph was just barely alive, and even though he turned to look at who was doing the hollering his eyes were too dim to be able to see him. He asked Half a Bob, "Who's that?"

"That's the Teal kid ya tried to shoot in Huntley."

"He's here? What's he doing here?"

"Same thing we are I guess, from the way he's been handled I'd say he's a captive just like us."

"He sure totes a grudge don't he?"

"I told ya not to work for Adolph any more, there's a bad sickness in his head; he don't think right anymore."

"Well if I could do it over again I wouldn't try to shoot him; I'd be best friends with him."

"Ya won't be making jokes after them redskins decide how we're going to die."

"Bob, I'm sorry I got ya into this mess, as for me I'm dead anyway, I hurt so bad I wish I was dead now."

"How about later Joseph? After we're dead? What happens then?"

"I wish we had a preacher here to help us get ready for whatever's coming; but I figure it's too late for us Bob, we made our choices a long time ago."

Matt had been straining to hear and had heard most of it, "ya no good back shoot 'n bushwhackers I hope ya rot in Hell." The rage he felt showed plainly in his eyes.

Bob looked at Matt, "what about you Mister Teal? Are you ready to die?"

CHAPTER SEVENTEEN

The Chief came and stood in front of Matt. "I want him made well; you make him better."

Matt glared at him, "I have hunted him for months now; it is my duty to kill him and you know that."

"We have many more reasons to kill him than you do. We are going to kill him our way; I want him well enough to last long time dying."

Matt just glowered, he knew he had no way of saying no and still live; that chief seemed pretty set on killing the two of them the hard way. His brothers would most likely think that was all right. If he lived to tell them about it! But he was not going to give in easy.

"Why should I do anything for you? You're my enemy and letting them braves beat me and kick me even drag me through the brush; I hunted him, I found him, I shot him and I have a right to kill him. I am not going to doctor him!"

"White boy do not anger me or I will give you much pain!"

"Do it! You can't keep me captive and expect me to help you, I helped you when you were hurt and you treat me this

145

way, I will do nothing for you! The Great Spirit will remember how you treated me and when you go to him he will repay."

He stared at Matt a long time but Matt would not be stared down and finally he spoke, "You fix him as good as you can and I will set you free with your horse."

Matt nodded his head and said, "all right I'll do it."

He knew better than to question the Chief's word; he had almost asked how he could be sure the Chief would keep his word but proud as that Injun was that just might make him really mad.

Things moved quickly then; a place was made for Hatchet Face, or rather Joseph, as that was his real name. Half a Bob, or Bob, was cut loose to help Matt. They had three Injuns watching them like prison guards. Joseph had already been treated as best as he could be and all he really needed was rest and something for the pain so he could sleep. Matt hated him and surprised himself that he felt that much emotion; he had never experienced that kind of feelings before.

"Listen fella, you're the bushwhacker that shot my pa, Bruiser Teal, and I'm gonna see you die hard!"

Joseph looked curiously at him, "I never shot no man by the handle of Bruiser Teal, I knew who he was of course but I never took money to kill him. The man that shot Bruiser was Adolph; all I did was watch his back trail for him. There was three of you and I put lead in one of your brothers shoulder to make you back off. But I never killed nobody."

"I don't know any Adolph, I've never even heard of him" Matt's eyes narrowed into hard mean slits, "You're trying to lie out of it, you got no reason to lie now but that don't make no difference, you'd lie when you're dying."

"No, he ain't." Bob answered him. "We were hired to watch his back trail; I was off to the east side of the trail and Joseph had the west side and Adolph paid us fifty dollars apiece. He didn't kill your brother; all we were after was to get you to quit the trail."

Matt heard the ring of truth and almost believed him. But he just couldn't bring himself to let go of what he had believed for so long over so many miles. "Who's this Adolph? And why was ya shooting at me in Huntley?"

"Adolph was a sharp shooter with us in the war and I shot at you to get you off my trail; you was hounding me so close I couldn't hardly move and then Adolph offered me two hundred dollars to take care of you and I could kill two birds with one shot, so's to speak."

"Even if that was so, you was part of it no matter who done the shooting."

"That's so," admitted Bob. "But the difference is we didn't even know who he was after until he'd made his shot. We were waiting out by the trail and he never told us anything until he rode by on the way to Mexico. There's no point in lying to you now; that's the way it was and that's the truth."

Matt would have to mull that over, it was like changing horses in the middle of the stream and it would take some thought.

Matt said "Well, we can let that go for now but we got to get loose from here in a hurry, they want to hang you upside down over a fire, Apache style, and Joseph you can't run yet so you sleep. But if we get loose I expect you to lead me to Adolph. Savvy?"

"We ain't gonna get loose from here; the best we can get out of it is a quick death. I sure ain't partial to hanging upside down screaming my lungs out and praying to die. If by some miracle we do get away we'll give you Adolph; more than that we'll help you catch him. We'll owe you our lives." Bob's voice was sincere and more and more Matt was starting to believe them.

Joseph had his head lying across his arms supported by his upraised knees; he had given up and was hopelessly dejected.

"We have a good chance of making it," Matt declared. "I'm going to cook these fellers a meal they won't forget. Bob you come over here and take care of Joseph." He pulled a tobacco sack from his saddlebags. "Just a little extra seasoning and they will love it."

He spread out his soogan and began pulling cooking pans from his possibles bag and laying them on it; then he set out a small cured ham and some spuds. He kept going until he had exposed every bit of food that he had, even his biscuit flour. It was all laying up close to the fire, curious braves crowded in close to watch what he was doing. They were getting in his way so much he had to step around them and they wanted to handle everything. He started doing every movement with a flourish.

He waved the salt around his head and made up grunts and special noises just for them. This was all very curious and they watched with more intensity. He chunked up a lot of fresh killed deer and rolled out all his biscuits dough on a flat rock; and soon had biscuits baking. Even the Chief was interested in his way of fixing things, and when he had the stew heating he emptied the tobacco sack of it's seasoning in the mix. Rosa had taken a lot of time making this stuff; there were all kinds of different plants that she knew about. First, she dried them, even the little red berries, then she used a large stone bowl and a round rock and she mashed it so fine she could sift it with her flour sifter. He set a young brave to watching it, stepped back, dug into his saddlebag again, and come back to the fire with a bottle of bootleg made just before he left German town. Tucker had bought three bottles and Matt had put a bottle in his things. He emptied the whole bottle into the stew hurriedly before any of them braves saw it.

There weren't anything left after those injuns finished eating; the Chief had gobbled down three bowls himself. "That sure must of been good," said Bob, he was looking forlorn and hungry. "It sure smelled good."

"Ya wouldn't have wanted any of that Bob, it would make you sleep and then make you really really sick".

At hearing that, Joseph rose up, "Ya mean we're going to make it?"

"Yup!" Matt sat down by him "When they sleep we'll tie them up and pick up everything that shoots, and when they wake up we'll use that lye soap to make soapy water and pour it down their throats; that will empty their guts. They'll be feeling too bad to make any problems and we'll take their horses and ride away." He added, "That Chief has got something coming to him and I'm gonna see to it that he gets it."

Matt heard a rustling noise in the brush that bordered their camp and he turned to investigate; there was King hiding not ten feet from him. He looked King square in the eyes and said, "I reckon you'd best get back to Tucker."

Only to find Tucker stretched out in the brush right beside King.

"I got this handled, move back a-ways," he said, just like he was talking to Bob.

"Huh? Bob looked puzzled, "What are you doing?"

"I'm telling Tucker and that big white dog of mine to back on out of here."

Joseph set up straight, "Ya ain't got that man killer here; have you? He don't take to me at all. He purt near bit my arm off; he'd of killed me if he could have reached me. Please keep him away from me!"

"That was then, with you running; now he won't bother you, it's a different critter entirely."

"I sure do hope he knows that!" Joseph looked around fretfully, "Where's he at now?"

"He's hiding in the brush with my brother; it's them injuns he'll be after, not you."

After a while them injuns where dropping down just about anywhere and was snoring loudly, Matt sincerely hope there wouldn't be no Apaches come by, all of them a - snoring was making a bunch of noise. Quietly Tucker and King came into the camp; everybody but Joseph was busy using their pigging strings tying up them redskins. Matt already had water on the fire with a bar of lye soap in it.

"We need to get their guts emptied out or they could die." He explained.

Joseph said, "I don't see nothing wrong with that, in fact let's hang that Chief upside down over the fire!"

Nobody answered him, mostly because they figured he was just blowing off smoke. Matt was busy dissolving the soap, he wanted to make sure nobody died if he could help it. He didn't know what to do with them, if he took them to German Town, they'd hang them. He didn't want to turn them loose because they'd most likely look for other white folks to kill. It might be best to just let them die, but it went against everything that he was, as a Teal and as a man. He turned to Tucker, "What do we do with them?"

"Take their Cayuse's and their guns and turn them loose to walk back to Mexico. They'll be shamed and laughed at, that's a big come down for any injun. Don't give them a canteen or food, if they make it, that'll be their good fortune, if the Apache gets them so much the better, that way we won't be killers."

"So be it." agreed Matt.

The soap suds emptied them out and they were sick puppies. Some were laying in their vomit. Some had emptied at both ends and were laying in all of it. Matt didn't untie them but let them wallow in their own mess. He remembered being spit on and kicked and hit when he was tied up. So he looked around for a good sized limb and when he found it he beat them all black and blue, especially the Chief.

"How strong is your medicine now?" He yelled at him.

The Chief had withstood the mistreatment stoically, without a yelp or groan or let own in any way he was hurting. Then Matt couldn't do no more, he even admired the way the Chief withstood him.

"White boy want kill me?" he asked and a small groan escaped him in spite of his determined effort to not make a sound.

"No," answered Matt. "I don't believe Great Spirit through with you yet. You didn't get a lick you didn't deserve. Ya turned on me when all I'd ever done was try to help you, and then bragged on yourself that you were strong. That's not being strong; you're just lying to yourself when ya try to believe that. A good man, white or Injun knows how to be loyal to family and even other people so there is trust between them. All you believe in is doing what you believe helps you no matter what's right. I bet if you see your pa in the spirit world he'll know what to do with you!"

He could see the Chief kind of shrivel up when he threw that bit about the Chief's Pa at him. They had the horses loaded with all the guns and knives; all the food and canteens, and were leaving them Kickapoo's a-foot and almost helpless. For the first, time the Chief looked defeated.

"You were stronger than I thought; I will think on the things we spoke about. I thank you for not killing us; I would like the gun you gave me."

Matt glared at him, "I bet you would, you'd most likely try to shoot me with it. We are enemies remember! I was willing for us to get along with each other once but that ain't gonna happen after what ya just put me through. I will not give you the rifle because I am strong and because I am strong I am letting you live, Injun!"

As they staggered away south Matt wondered about their fate especially the Chief. He had a strong feeling this was not the last time he would see him.

Half a Bob said he knew where Adolph was because another friend had saw him just a while back, and he wasn't in Old Mexico but was headed north to the high plains! The trail was going to be a long one and Hatchet Face as Matt still called him, couldn't make the trip in his condition. It was decided that Tucker would take him back to the ranch and have them lock him up till they had everyone that was involved in Bruiser's shooting together. Matt and Half a Bob along with King would go on after Adolph. Tucker had promised Bob a free ticket out of Texas and promised him five hundred dollars for helping catch Adolph, so that he would be on their side and not betray Matt as soon as he had opportunity. Matt wasn't worried about what he could do but Tucker wanted the extra carrot in Bob's eyes to spur him in the right direction. Besides these fellers had a code they lived by; once they had taken money for the job, they'd not back down from it. Half a Bob didn't believe Adolph had quit on the job he'd took to kill the Teals; "He might be just letting things cool down first." That was the way he figured it.

They had let Tucker worry about all the stuff they'd took from the Kickapoo's and had their mounts and a pack horse. Bob turned southwest and commented, "We're apt to be on a long road to catch this feller, but I know his stomp 'n grounds and we'll find him."

As it turned out it was getting to be a long road; they'd been checking places where Adolph might be found for what seemed like months and still not a clue. They was at the biggest cave Matt had ever seen, they was in rolling hills in limestone country and camped where they could watch the cave.

"Bob we ain't get 'n no closer and I'm beginning to think you're stonewalling me. If you are I'm gonna hang you out to dry; I guarantee it!"

Bob shook his head, "I was sure he'd come back to one of these places. Let's head towards Amarillo; sometimes he goes up there to stay within riding distance of a lady friend that likes his money. Pack up, lets head that way." By late evening, they had covered just about twenty miles and figured it must be time for coffee and beans. They were set 'n back, Bob was scraping his pipe bowl and thinking on a smoke, and Matt was restringing a bow he'd kept, one that the Chief had been using. Suddenly Bob had disappeared in the brush away from the fire; Matt froze in place, he was alert with all his senses searching for the reason Bob had disappeared. The big white dog had both ears standing up and his whole body tensed and ready, but his eyes were probing the late evening light. At the same time he was aware of Matt and waiting for a command from him.

"Hello the camp."

King voiced a low menacing rumble from way down in his throat; Matt laid a hand on his head to shush him.

"Come on in if you're a mind to," Matt hollered back. "If'n you're friendly you'll be ok if'n you're not ya best ride on."

"We're friendly," was the comeback; and a couple of cowboys walked their horses into the firelight. "We smelled that coffee a long ways back; ya must not be afraid of injuns."

Matt passed the tin cups around, "Help yourselves to the coffee, you're too late for supper, but we got some fixings if'n ya want to eat."

"Coffee's fine for us, we ate a while back." They hunkered down on their heels and sipped at the hot Arbuckle's. "The brew o the west," one of the strangers laughed.

"What would we do without Arbuckle's coffee and red eye gravy?"

"I reckon life wouldn't be the same alright," Matt agreed. "You fellers headed on west?"

"We're thinking on Amarillo, there's a chance we might latch on to a cattle drive from there." The cowhand got to his feet; he was tall, skinny, and in his thirty's, the other hand was built like him but younger. They weren't twins but they looked alike.

"We're the Barnes's from over east of San Antonio; we're brothers." which pretty well explained their resemblance to each other.

King pushed by Matt and stood silently staring at them, the rumble of displeasure still in his throat.

"Well I'll swan if'n ya don't have my dog, my name ain't Elmer if that ain't him. Come here Jack," and he snapped his fingers. "Get over here right now or I'll whip your hide off."

"That's my dog and you reach for a whip I'll use it on you!"

"I guess I know my own dog mister and he is my dog and I'm taking him.'"

"Ya ain't touching him." Matt's voice was angry. "King is mine and I'd never let you get your hands on him."

Elmer stepped towards King and he growled a warning and showed his teeth, Elmer jumped back "You growling at me, well I'll show you whose boss and he grabbed a quirt from off his saddle. When he did King leaped at him and ripped his arm with his enormously big teeth.

Elmer had blood running down his arm and a long deep gash clear to the bone. Elmer's brother grabbed his gun but let it go when he saw the gun Bob had trained on him.

"It appears to me you fellers need to be riding on." Bob was speaking soft but his tone of voice was menacing. "King don't seem to like you and he has decided to stay with us."

"That's my dog and I'll be back for him," threatened Elmer.

"Feller my name is Matt Teal and if you want to die over a dog, you help yourself."

Elmer's face changed color to slightly pale "You Teals think you're so high and mighty but this is one time you're gonna lose! He's my dog and I'm gonna take him."

The tension around the camp fire was putting a real strain on everybody standing there; so much so that it had become a matter of pride, and horse sense was in short supply. Bob stepped closer to Elmer "At this distance there's no chance at all for either of us; we'll both die! Now I don't see much about that dog worth dying for; He don't even like you. So before I'll die for him I'm gonna shoot him; it's better for him to die than it is for me to get killed over him. Or is it even about the dog? Maybe it's just you being gun proud. Ya see that boy over there; with him it is about the dog! He really loves that dog; but you don't even like the dog and he hates you, and you are just determined not to be outdone. I'll tell you something, I believe it is your dog and Matt knows it's your dog, it's just that, that dog saved his life awhile back and he's grateful. Would you sell the dog? I'll give you twenty dollars for him."

By this time Elmer was madder than an old wet hen, but his brother who still could think straight said right out, "We'll sell him! I ain't getting' in no gun fight over that blame dog. We'll take the twenty dollars for him."

Bob reached in his pocket and passed him one of the gold pieces he'd got from Tucker.

"It's a done deal."

"I ain't selling my dog." Elmer yelled.

"Shut up, I done sold him, and we need the money, or have ya forgot we're riding the grub line."

"I ain't giving up my dog! Elmer yelled at him.

But that was all he said, his brother hit him so hard on the chin he was lucky not to have a broken jaw. When he woke up he was too far away to cause any more trouble, and by then his arm was in bad shape and needed attention which took his mind off King or Jack as he called him.

"Twenty dollars was a lot of money for a dog," criticized Matt "Twenty dollars was cheap compared to our lives." Returned Bob calmly, knowing that Matt was looking for something to peck about. "Let's get shut of this place afore that cowboy gets awake and heads back here."

CHAPTER EIGHTEEN

"Ya know," Matt said, "I'm purely flummoxed if'n I can make sense outta the man, I think he just wanted to make King give in. He didn't want him; he wanted to force him to beg or something."

"King ain't the kind to give in and he'll hate that man forever," Bob told him.

"I reckon that part's so," echoed Matt, "My brother Cord is a lot like that; Pa would take his razor strap to us and I'd yell real loud cause I knew he'd quit sooner if I did. Cord wouldn't make a sound and Pa would just whip him harder, got so Pa hated to whip Cord because he was so stubborn."

They rode on quiet for a while each lost in his own thoughts. King ran alongside of Mouse, no one could figure his thoughts but if they could, ole Elmer needed to worry about where King was. They come on a wagon train circled up on the outskirts of Amarillo and Luther ran to meet Matt.

Bob purt near grinned he was so shot with luck; he said, "That's your man a-coming there." And then he called, "Hello Adolph."

Luther looked at Bob puzzled and turned to Matt. "Who's he? And why is he calling me Adolph?"

Matt faced Bob, "I know this man and he ain't Adolph."

"I know him too; I went through the war with him. He is Adolph and he's the one who shot your pa."

A pretty young lady ran from the wagons to Luther sliding her arm through his; she was all smiles and giggles, "Hi Matt, did you come for our wedding?"

Matt was shocked, puzzled and unsure of what to do or say, but Bob was sure; he had Luther covered and his hand was steady as a rock.

"Adolph, I hate to do this to you but I been hired to find you and I've done that. We're taking you back to Two Track, to stand trial for killing Bruiser Teal."

Matt stared at Luther; Luther's face had twisted, his eyes were bulging out and his chin quivered. "Ahaa" he uttered and he fell to the ground. He'd turned ghostly white, while his breath came in gasps like a man choking. Imogene screamed and screamed; her pa and others come a-running, whilst Bob wisely holstered his colt. J.T. took command and they laid Luther in one of the wagons and the women were waiting for him to come too. J.T. turned on Matt, "Did you do anything to cause him to pass out like that?"

Misery showed through Matt's eyes, "I reckon so." He said simply without explaining.

"You care to enlarge on that? We'd like to hear more than just; I reckon so."

Bob could see Matt wasn't up to saying nothing else. "Luther ain't Luther a-tall, his real name is Adolph and he's a killer for hire."

J. T. could see Matt was suffering and studied him a mite before saying, "You believe that?"

Matt shook his head no and then said, "I don't believe it. There's something hay wire about this."

"He don't want to believe it, Adolph killed his pa and then fate threw them together and now he's finding out folks are never all bad or all good and Bob smirked, "he's having a bad time with this. He'll be alright, he's made of the right stuff and he'll come out of it just fine." Bob placed his hand condescendingly on Matts shoulder.

Matt twisted his shoulder to push Bob's hand off.

"Just how do you fit into this?" J.T. asked, "Do ya know this feller you call Adolph?"

"I know him; we served in the same company in the war." Bob didn't spell out just exactly what they did in the army. "I think he got twisted from all the killing. He got so mean everybody tried to stay away from him."

"He sure don't show any sign of meanness now and he's been with us long enough we'd a-knowed if'n he was a bad 'n. I just don't believe ya."

"You are calling me a liar?"

"Stop it Bob! You drag iron and I'll kill ya." Matt was ready, his hand was hovering over the pearl grips of his colt. "He's got a right to be unsure of what you're saying."

Bob made himself relax and he straightened up. "I reckon so." He admitted, "I'm touchy about things like that."

"If he's what ya say he is then you can take him, but before we let him go we're going to know a whole lot more about this." J. T. was adamant and his voice was real strong; it were plain how he felt about Luther. It was for sure that he felt unconvinced and perturbed; and he weren't gonna be easy to convince.

"For one thing," J.T. kept on. "I'm not sure what axe you got to grind your own self. You might have some reason besides the truth for claiming he's this Adolph you say he is."

Matt was paying real close heed to J.T. because he felt the man was making sense. But still he couldn't figure Bob lying when he had nothing to gain by it. Did Bob just pick Luther willy nilly? But that wouldn't work because what if he picked a man that'd been with the train since the start. So at the very least he had to know Luther was new to the wagon train; and how could Bob know that because he'd been taking care of Joseph all that time? Matt was uneasy about saying Luther was guilty but there was a lot that pointed to him being what Bob said he was.

J.T. wasn't sure either and he decided, "What we're going to do is have a council; everybody on the train is going to hear both sides and make a decision; and that will be what we'll do, no more argument."

Well Matt was in favor of that and even Bob seemed to feel like that was a good way to go about it. What Matt didn't know was Bob intended to take Luther back no matter what was decided. Matt walked with Luther out away from camp so they could have a private talk. "I'm guessing ya got your memory or part of your memory back; didn't you?" he gave Luther a hard look that didn't leave any room for denial.

"I remember some things about the war and there's not much else that I can recall that went on before that, but I can remember how much Bob and Joseph was scared I would tell about what they had done. But I can't remember the other things that I did or even where I've been."

"What had they done that they didn't want ya to tell?"

"I can't think of what it was; I've been trying to, but I just can't bring it back."

"That ain't gonna help much, they'll just say that you're making that stuff up and ya got no way of proving anything. But at least, now I know how he picked you out when we rode up. Ya can't trust Bob no-how nor no-ways, I think he'll find an excuse to kill you if'n he gets you alone; ya need to run and stay hid till I get a handle on the truth that I can prove. Ya get a couple of broncs and some grub together and be gone afore morning. Go to San Antonio, keep outta sight till I get this settled, put up at the Menger Hotel and don't walk around looking the town over; don't go no further than the Lockwood saloon. The more you show yourself the more risk you run."

"What if I get my memory back and I'm guilty?"

"Then ya come on in and give yourself up."

"Have you that much faith in me?"

"I reckon I do, ya take care of yourself and don't ya tell anybody about your leaving; I mean anybody; ya hear me?"

"She won't tell," Luther started to say but Matt broke in, "I said don't tell and ya got to pay attention if'n you're going to live."

Luther took Matt's hand, "If I did it, I'll come and give myself up; I give ya my word."

Matt shook his hand, "I do trust you; Have ya got enough money?"

"I don't have any money at all; I guess I lost it when I got caught in that flash flood."

Then Matt remembered about the money he'd taken from him when he was purt near dead. He reached in his saddle bag and searched out the wallet he'd took off of him, he'd been carrying it ever since. He smiled kind of sheepishly and handed it to him.

"Here, I forgot this, there's enough in there to keep you for a-while."

Matt and Bob slept out away from the wagons whilst Luther rolled up his bedroll close to Imogene's wagon. Well after midnight Matt heard horses moving softly out into the night and smiled when he knew Luther was gone and had not been challenged. It was the smell of coffee that brought him awake the next morning; he glanced at Bob who was snoring lightly and tried not to wake him. The morning sun was just peeking up over the horizon and while it was still mostly dark there was coffee brewing and fresh side bacon cooking along with biscuits and red eye gravy. The fire was crackling and sparks were flying away in the slight breeze and peace reigned. Matt sighed and set up; all kinds of uproar was gonna happen in just a little bit and he should get a cup of coffee first if'n he could. He lucked out, there was not only fresh coffee but some cold biscuits from last night's supper was left on a pan close by. J.T. was already set 'n there holding his big tin cup with both his large hands wrapped around it. The smile he greeted Matt with was more reflective than his regular good morning smile.

"Help yourself, son. It's fresh just this morning."

Matt found a space on the same log J.T. was squat 'n on. "I reckon I'll just do that J.T., everything is quiet this morning."

"That's generally when ya need to be on guard the most; that's just the lull before the storm."

They both gave a chuckle at that. Matt remembered his pa used to say that.

"It's too nice a morning to be spoilt by a storm." He pointed towards the tree line, "Look over there." A mule deer was grazing along paying them no mind. "Maybe ya could get that big white dog of your 'n to go bring him down."

"Ain't he purty, I seen him earlier but I don't want to wake the camp by shooting him. But if'n I sent King after him he'd have him ate before we could get to him."

J.T. chuckled over that, "That deer would just about fill him up I guess."

Matt went back to his possibles bag and found his moccasins; and silently slipped into the brush followed by King. J. T. watched with interest; he took out his sack of Bull Durham and tamped more tobacco in the bowl of his pipe. He had no idea what the boy had in mind. But he kept watching and in a little while Matt showed in the tree line very close to the buck.

Then the buck started to run and ended up pushing his nose into the dirt. "Well I'll swan," swore J.T. as he headed for Matt and where King was nosing the downed deer.

"I'd heard about slings before but I've never seen it done before. I'm gonna learn me how to do that."

J.T. purt near strutted whilst helping carry that buck back to the wagons. "Them folks will be surprised when they get up to have deer neck steaks for breakfast this morning." He busily sliced off both neck loins and was cutting them into small neck steaks.

Matt laughed but he felt a little bit important, covered as he was with praise from J.T. Matt sat on a log holding a tin cup of coffee and watched the breakfast being cooked. The smells were making him hungry; hot biscuits, lightly browned, fluffy and ready for butter made his mouth water. He had temporarily forgotten Luther and set there unconcerned and happy till Half a Bob come running hollering something about Luther being gone. Matt looked at him confused by the sudden change from contentment to confusion he had totally let Luther slip out of his thoughts and was jolted back to reality by Bobs yells.

"He's run! He's got away!"

Well that got everybody looking in and around things; "he's gone" was the general consensus. Everybody must of said that at least twice, "He's gone alright."

Bob got in Matt's face and yelled, "I told you we ought 'a tie him up; I did didn't I?"

Matt tried to look sheepish so's they wouldn't catch on; but it was too obvious to hide and soon they were accusing him of sett' n Luther free.

"Wait just a blame minute," bellowed J.T. "He never set that kid free; use your heads, the boy was never tied up to start with; Matt didn't have' ta set him free. We all trusted him and maybe we shouldn't have and now he's gone; but we're as much to blame as Matt."

"You!" he pointed at Half a Bob, "you could've guarded him so don't be blaming someone else; ya could've watched him and your just as much to blame as anyone else."

"Let's go find him." Bob grabbed at Matts arm excitedly.

Matt shook his hand off, "We got something more important to do first; he can wait, he ain't going very far away from Imogene. While we're this close I want to pick up whoever paid for pa's killing. We'll bring in that person and pa's killer at the same time."

That wasn't what Bob wanted to do and Matt had to get firm with him but finally they set out to go get the person who paid for Bruiser's shooting. It took a-while to get loose from the wagon train, and everybody had an opinion about Luther and wanted to tell Matt what they thought he ought to do. Bob was fidgety and wanted to leave so he just rode off and Matt had to catch up.

"There weren't no need to be so rude." Matt told him, "We had time to say a proper goodbye."

"I get paid for bringing in the ones Tucker is paying me for; not to palaver all day getting gone. We already lost Adolph and now we'll have to hunt him down again."

"Finding Luther or Adolph as you call him ain't gonna be a problem, answered Matt angrily, "I don't believe he had any part of pa's death. If'n I find ya been leading me down the primrose path we will have a reckoning. I told you that once before."

"Kid, I took Tuckers money to bring him in and I will bring him in. I know him for what he is and you don't, he's got you hornswoggled and blinded to what he is; he is a killer. He's twisted and is as mean a varmint as you'll ever meet. Ya won't believe me yet but you'll see before this is all over; I guarantee that you'll see him for what he is."

"Right now I've got my doubts; if'n I'm wrong I'll be there pulling on the rope that hangs him. Let's go get the ones that hired my pa's killing and we'll get back on the killers trail."

Bob touched his spurs to his horse; he moved out in front to lead off. Three long hard days of travel got them close to the Llano River and Matt was ready to eat someone else's cooking and sleep in a real bed.

"Junction is that way? Is that where we're headed?" Matt asked?

"Yep, we'll be headed up the Llano after we cross at Junction; the ones ya want has a place out that way."

"I smell smoke," Matt stood in his stirrups and tried to spot where it was coming from.

Bob sniffed the air, "Ya got a good nose, and I smell it now that you've mentioned it. In this hill country a small fire in the bottom of one of these ravines will be hard to spot."

"I think it's over that a way," Matt pointed. A wisp of smoke blown about by the wind was faintly visible, dissolving into nothingness and surprising them because of its closeness. Bob pulled up, "We've almost walked into a trap of some kind; let's move back and circle. You go to the right and I'll go left. Whoever is hiding in there will have to move and we'll have him."

Matt nodded and reined Mouse to his right moving slow and nerves on edge, his body tensed and ready to draw. They had just started when those hiding stood up and just stood there waiting. Matt turned Mouse right towards them.

"It's them blame Kickapoo's again; about twenty of'm." He hollered at Bob. And facing the chief he asked, "What in tarnation is going on?"

The chief gave him that roguish grin; "we need get back twenty horses."

"Get back? What happened to your horses?"

"We lose them in horse race with Apaches, they bring this sorry ugly Cayuse that did not look like it could last the distance of a race and want race with us. So we put our fastest pony in race with our best rider and their ugly, laughable, broken down, crow bait ran off and left our rider in dust. We lose all our horses, now we can't go back to village walking again; I would be laughed at and there would be a different chief. They get another."

Bob laughed, "Ya think we care? After what you did to us? We are enemies; we will kill you and sell your scalps."

The chief stood erect and a cloak of dignity seemed to cover him. "Yes, you would but Matt much warrior and would not."

Matt didn't like the way Bob was trying to make his decisions for him and resented it.

"I believe chief much warrior and as warrior to warrior I will give you thirty horses from our ranch at Two Track."

Bob was sputtering he was so mad. "You will not; Tucker wouldn't even let you."

"I own as much of that ranch as Tucker or any of the rest of my brothers and they cannot stop me. We have more horses than you can count and I will give him thirty horses. There's no need for him to lose his place in the tribe, I might kill him in battle the next time I see him but I won't let him be disgraced as a warrior."

Matt felt a little foolish because he really didn't care what happened to the Kickapoo Chief but he wasn't gonna let Bob run things. Besides it sounded kind of like something one of the knights of old might of done. The stories his ma used to read him of knights doing grand things. He wondered for a minute about what had happened to that book? He faced the Kickapoo Chief, "We are on our way to capture those that paid gold for someone to kill my pa. Ya wait close to here and we'll be back and we'll go get your horses."

"See," said the chief. "My power much greater than yours or you would not give me horses." And then he laughed.

Matt glared and then smiled, "Ya ain't getting under my skin, you just be here when I get back. Understand?"

CHAPTER NINETEEN

They rode off towards Junction and Matt wasn't sure why he'd promised that old rascal anything. His pa would've said it was kid stuff. It didn't matter now; he'd said it and he'd do it. He wondered how much his brothers were gonna charge him for them Cayuses. They might think it was funny and take it easy on him unless Jake would figure he needed a lesson and then it might get expensive.

Another day and they were there; looking down on a well-kept ranch house and corrals. They just watched for a while; there weren't no ranch hands in sight and that was in their favor.

"Let's just go on down there and knock on their door." suggested Matt.

"We can do that alright," Bob was doubtful, "but we might be better off to set tight for a bit and see if they're both at home. It might be one of them is gone and then we'd have just one and the other' n might get wind of it and run."

So they hid and watched, the hours going by until they were tired, when finally a buggy drove in, it was carrying the man and woman that had stopped at Two Track.

"I remember them," Matt whispered to Bob, "are ya sure them's the ones?"

"These folks paid money to Adolph to kill every Teal on the ranch."

"Let's go get them." Matt was ready to move, his anger was barely under control. "Them farmers has got a rope coming to them."

"Let me go first; they'll recognize me as being with Adolph. You pull your hat down over your face more and try to stay where they can't see you real well."

And that's the way they rode in. When they were close enough to see faces, the woman recognized Bob and waved a welcome. Bob let his arm dangle by his side and twisted sideways a little gathering his colt in his hand, only when they were real close did he point the six gun at them. She was so surprised when she recognized Matt she jumped back a step and her hand covered her mouth and her husband stared at Matt, mouth open.

"What's he doing here?" her voice quivered.

"Never mind him, ya stand real still if ya want to live because if you move, I'll kill ya." Bob's hard tone of voice both startled them and confirmed he meant business.

"Where's the other woman?" Matt asked.

"My ma died just a little while after you people killed my pa; she didn't want to live with him gone."

"Why are you here?" The woman's voice was subdued and shaky. Bob answered her. "We are here on law business; you two are under arrest for hiring a killer to kill the Teal family."

"Just whose side are you on?" You was here with Adolph when we paid him and now you're back saying we're under arrest. That don't make sense! I thought you were on our side." Bud's fright had changed to anger.

"I'm on my own side, and right now I'm getting paid to bring you in."

"All right," the woman said. "How much too just walk away."

"Lady when I take money to do a job there ain't no amount of money going to buy me."

"You already took money from us, so according to your own lights you can't sell us out." Her voice was firmer now and Matt could see she thought she had him. "I never took your money and I didn't share in Adolph's promise to you," Bob said. "You are going back to Two Track to face judgment. Get some of your stuff together; it's going to be a long ride; all the way back to Two Track where you'll stand trial."

Matt stared at the woman, was this the same one that had been the object of so much admiration outside the "Red Eye." She was different now. Her face was pinched and bitter looking, her eyes were belligerent and sullen. Outside the saloon at "Two Track" she had been an object of admiration but look at her now. Look how much bitterness had changed her.

Matt had kept his horse turned where he could watch the cook shack and the bunk house but so far no hands had shown up. He asked Bud. "Where's your hands?"

"We ain't got but two and they live close enough to just ride over every morning when we need them. They come and do the milking and put out feed and water."

"Have ya got one that you can put in charge of the place?"

"I reckon so; I really need to get things together if we're not coming back."

Matt nodded, "We'll let you get things squared away before we take you."

"Like blazes," Bob yelled. "They didn't let Bruiser have time to get thing squared away and they ain't gonna have time to get a rescue organized whilst we are getting them to "Two Track.""

Matt stared at Bob with a hard unyielding look in his eye until Bob looked away. "Go on," Matt told them, "get your stuff together."

Silently they laid out their bed rolls and food stuffs, some clean clothes and water bags, but Bob was at their heels every step until they were in their saddles and moving. The house had been closed up and the morning chores taken care of, Matt even let them leave a note for the hired man they were leaving in charge. They had a half a dozen mounts in a corral so Matt brought them along for the Kickapoo's to ride and they were glad to get them.

"Much tired of walking." The Chief told Matt.

King had ran up to the Chief to be petted, Matt laughed, "For some reason he's always liked you."

The chief scratched the big dog's ears, "I like him, and so he likes me. I have good thoughts for you so you have good thoughts for me; even so we be warriors." Matt thought that pretty well explained why he'd given him the horses and felt the better for it.

For some reason their friendliness seemed to anger Half a Bob and he shouted, "We got a long way to go; so let's get to it."

"Are you going to give back our guns now?" The chief had that roguish look again, so Matt knew he was being provoked but it angered him anyway.

. "Do I look like a fool to you? Did ya think that pretty little speech about us being warriors together softened my brain? I'll never trust you again; I tried being nice to you and look at what you did? No never again."

"I only try to bring smile; I not fool." The chief stared straight into his eyes.

Matt felt foolish, he knew he'd been cranky when there hadn't been any call for it. So there was only silence between them as they rode. They had six horses and there were twenty or so Indians so they took as many as they had horses for and the rest had to stay behind and wait till they brought more horses. Most days Bob headed them up and Matt rode beside the Chief; the truth was he kind of liked the old reprobate. He had a funny side to him and every once in a while he was good for a laugh. It was a puzzle how he could be so jovial and easy going and still be the savage that Matt knew he was. Matt had no illusions as to what he was but he had to admit sometimes the Chief could be likeable.

It had been a long weary trek when one night Bob slipped away and left Matt with the Ward's and the Kickapoo's. Matt was angry; he was sure that Bob had taken off to find Luther. But there was nothing could be done about it now.

"Chief, Bob has taken off to go find a man he thinks was the one that killed my pa so I'm going to need you people to help me get the Wards back to "Two Track.""

"If he tries to get Adolph away from my people they'll take his scalp." The Chief grinned. "There's no one can get him from my people."

Matt reined Mouse to a halt. "What did you say about Adolph being at your camp?"

"I say he our prisoner and no one take."

"You have Adolph? Are you sure? What does he look like?"

The Kickapoo laughed, "I have him, he look like Brother Joseph that you take captive."

"Joseph has a brother?"

"Why you think strange Joseph have brother?"

Matt didn't know why he hadn't thought about that slant; all of a sudden he could see why Bob and Joseph had been so determined to place the blame on Luther, they was protecting Adolph.

"That changes everything," Matt exclaimed excitedly.

"You no give horses now?" The chief was concerned.

"I will give you the horses and cows and much money, you give me Adolph and you can have gifts beyond you've ever dreamed!"

"I cannot give you Adolph, the tribe would kill me."

"There will be a hundred men with many weapons to take him from you, Jake won't fool around he'll just shoot you and go get Adolph."

He just stood there stubbornly shaking his head no. Matt drew the fastest draw he had ever made and the bullet made a red line across the Chiefs left foot. Very solemnly he raised his foot, examined it and then he set it down and looked Matt in his eyes. "I think we can make deal."

"Chief, your braves will be much happy with you. I will give you the best rifle ever made; it will look like a Chiefs rifle. There will be four more but they won't look like a Chief's rifle."

"I will hold my new rifle in my hands while I burn and my people are dragging much wood up for heap big fire."

"You think they'll be angry when a hundred cows are being watched over by your young men, and in your tepees there are many blankets. There will be one hundred horses to choose from to ride, and much gold to buy pots, salt, and much pretty cloth for your wives."

Matt could see the war chief wavering. "Your camp will be richest camp of all other tribes. Your name will be famous everywhere. Just exactly what is your name?'

"My name is Matunaaga; in your language it means "He fights" I get name at birth."

"I better just call ya Chief, famous for having "plenty of horses.""

The Chief nodded, "I think maybe this is so, I will call council and we will make talk. We will do much talk, listen to the one who sees in the spirit world, and bring you Adolph. You must bring big gift, very big gift for the medicine man and then he will shake his rattles over much smoke and look into smoke, do dance, shake rattles, look very grave and tell people to give Adolph to white eyes. I do not like medicine man."

Matt grinned, "I believe that, why not just get a different one. What do you call him anyway? "The chief tighten his jaw, "Eluwilussit or Holy one and one night he will walk out of camp and disappear, his body will not be found so it must be that the spirits have taken him."

Matt wanted to get things started so he laid it out, "I'm going to take my prisoners on to the ranch. You send some of your braves with me to get started gathering up a hundred horses and you bring Adolph to the ranch." Chief Matunaaga made a few motions and injuns started moving.

Matt said, "I got to learn how you do that; at the ranch I'd have to get their attention, and then repeat it twice, draw them a picture and still have to send someone with them to make sure it was done right."

He waved at the Chief as he and his braves left at a lope, whilst he worked at getting his own collection of hombres and King headed in the right direction. They headed southeast to pick up the San Antonio to Laredo road; it'd be lots faster traveling once they were on it. The Chief and his braves where headed southwest, while Matt had the Wards and four injuns to help guard them. He was a little worried about setting them Kickapoo's to guard a pair of White eyes. That'd be like setting old yeller to watch over a mouse. The one called Kitchi was the one left in charge and he looked like he could keep a tight rein on the others and a hundred more. He looked at me and grinned. His jaws was big enough to clamp down on the head of a cougar, about half of his teeth were gone, what was left looked to be about two inches long. His grin brought shivers up and down my back bone. I know enough to know not to show fear but whoever said that had never seen "He who Kills Enemies"

* * * *

Finding Luther was a lot easier than Half a Bob expected. Luther was in the lobby of the Menger Hotel, a five story elegant structure. Half a Bob walked up behind Luther, placed the barrel of his colt in his back and he had his man.

He didn't get the welcome he thought he would at the Teal ranch. Jake questioned him about where Matt was and why Matt didn't come in with him. And he questioned Luther. Putting all the information together it soon became obvious that Bob had run out on Matt hoping to get all the credit of the capture of the Wards, and his version of who Luther was. Jake decided Half a Bob was a liar and locked him up with Joseph. . Luther he let bunk in the bunkhouse.

* * * *

It was two weeks later before Matt and the Wards were at the ranch, King had run ahead to announce their arrival, Tucker saw King and his jaw dropped in amazement. "Matt's home", he hollered. The Wards were locked up and guarded. The Kickapoo's, a surprise, were settled by the creek. Teal men were gathered by the well to hear Matt's report.

"What do the Kickapoo's have to do with all of this?" Tucker asked. The wind was getting stronger and whipping the dirt and leaves around in small sporadic spirals spread across the yard.

"Let's get down in the well and get out of this wind." Jake was already on the step's that led inside the well.

Inside the well had the advantage of being free from the dirt whipping wind as well as the privacy from the workers.

"Wow, I'll tell a man if'n that ain't nasty out there." Tucker laughed and banged his hat again his knee. "I believe my feet were off the ground mor'n they was touching it."

"Alright let's get on with this, ya ready to tell us how it was Matt?

"Yes, but let's get to the kitchen table with some coffee in front of us."

So, tired as he was, Matt started at where he had left Tucker when Cord had been shot and he had followed the shooter. He covered it all including where he had pulled that dirt bank in on himself. He left out the fears and the tears but figured they knew anyway. They chuckled at his mistakes and gave their approval when he had done well. The hours slipped by and when he'd told it all it was past bed time and he was plumb worn out. Cord wanted to know if he could find his way back to the treasure and Jake wanted to know more about that hard shouldered jasper that had tried to bluff him out of his horses and seemed to know him.

Then his brothers had a surprise for him; with a lot of fanfare they declared him to be a top hand. Which they reminded him was ten dollars a month more money and they had enough gold coins to cover the months he'd been gone. Jake asked "How many of those rascals do we have?"

"We got the Wards, Joseph, and Half a Bob. That's four of them leaving one more."

"You should of shot them," Tucker said. "No one would have blamed you."

"I would have blamed me, if pa was alive he would have blamed me, you know how he felt about right and wrong."

"He was a stickler for being in the right; I don't guess any of us will forget that. The sheriff said that the judge only comes every two months and he was just here."

"What's gonna happen?" Matt asked, "Is the Sheriff going to take them to the jail? Or, are we going to make a place under guard for them on the ranch."

"We will hold them here until the Sheriff comes for them." Jake explained.

CHAPTER TWENTY

The next morning Matt went to find Luther and found him in the bunkhouse with the men. Matt smiled at him and sat down beside him. "You ok?"

"I am now; I thought they was going to lynch me before you got here to speak for me. I was scared out of my mind."

"I'm sorry that you had such a hard time and I know it had to be a hard thing to go through."

Matt looked inquiringly at him, "Do you remember your real name yet?"

Luther stuck out his hand to be shook, "Hi, I'm Algernon Frank."

Matt laughed, "I think I like Luther better."

"I'm so glad to be alive I don't care what I'm called."

"Do you remember what you were doing out here?"

"I was on my way to my Uncle's place to help him for a while. He fell and got hurt pretty bad so I was going to help. Then I ran into Bob and Joseph and stopped to talk with them. They must of shot me from behind while I was figuring on how to get across that Arroyo running with the flash flood. Then you pulled me out of that mess and saved my life."

181

He turned serious, "I owe you Matt and I don't have the right words to express how much I appreciate all you've done."

Matt grinned, "Your first born boy will be enough! Actually you'd of done the same thing for me. What's next? Are you going to hurry back to the wagon train?"

"I guess the first thing will be to let my folks know what happened. Then I'll make the decisions that affect the rest of my life. I'm not sure I'm ready for Imogene right at this point of time, I don't believe I'll be ready to have another person to be responsible for until a long time from now."

Matt took him by his hand, "You don't have to explain those things to me; I'll always be here for you, I am your friend forever." Matt walked back to the ranch house; he did not want to watch his friend leave.

The next morning Jake set the hands to bringing in horses and the Indians went with them to pick out what they wanted. "Much good." The Indian taking the lead waved his arm at the herd. They made their pick and were pleased with themselves. With the Indians happy, Jake sent for the Sheriff to start the process of justice for Bud and his wife; Bud said her name was Josephine.

The Sheriff came driving his buggy into the ranch yard followed by the jail house wagon. Jake explained to him who was involved. Half a Bob, Joseph, and the Wards were severely questioned and taken to jail in Two Track, with round the clock protection from the angry town folks.

Three days later the Chief and his medicine man, Eluwilussit, brought Adolph to the ranch for questioning by the Sheriff. Matt was astonished at how much Adolph and Joseph looked alike. "Them two are hard cases; they are about as bad as it's possible to get," Sam observed. Adolph was listening to Sam and smiled, "You're counting your chickens before they hatch. I did not kill anybody, the Wards will not admit to being involved in any such terrible act and you can't prove anything against us. You see in this country you have to prove I'm guilty; just because some big rancher wants to hang somebody and picked me, a decorated veteran, doesn't mean I'm guilty. Where's your witnesses who saw me shoot anyone? What evidence do you have?"

Sam turned to Jake and Matt, "did you hear that?" Jake had a thoughtful look on his face. "He just might be right. He'll play his medals and we'll be the big rich rancher trying to hang somebody."

Later the county attorney agreed with Adolph, "There's not much to work with without the Wards testimony and so far they are denying everything."

The Kickapoo Chief was much disturbed and said to Matt, "If you not hang him we kill him our way." Later on that afternoon Matt searched for the Chief but it appeared the Indians had gone back to their village. Matt understood how he must be feeling; there was no way that he could understand the white man's code of justice.

A few days later the Sheriff sat in his buggy and apologized to Matt. "I don't know what happened Matt, I went to the jail this morning, the jailor was tied up on the floor, Half a Bob was dead in his cell, The Wards were badly beaten and barely alive, Joseph and Adolph are missing. I suspect it was your Indian friends."

Matt nodded, "It's all right, I'll bet you they died the hard way." Matt felt drained, he felt like a wrung out dish rag and he turned and started for the house. When Sam fell in step beside him, "You did a really good job Matt. We are proud of you. I reckon it turned into a rough ole road?"

"Yeh," Matt said sardonically, "It was a Ten dollar Road."

Edwards Brothers Malloy
Oxnard, CA USA
February 12, 2016